Mark A. Radcliffe is the author of two novels, Gabriel's Angel (2010) and Stranger Than Kindness (2013), both published by Bluemoose and a collection of short stories, Superpowers (2020) published by Valley Press. He is currently the Subject Lead for Creative Writing at West Dean College of Art and Conservation. Prior to that he worked as a nurse, a health journalist/columnist and a senior lecturer in mental health practice and nursing.

Mark lives in Hove with his wife Kate and swims in the sea a lot. His daughter Maia does not swim in the sea a lot but is a faster swimmer than he is anyway. He's ok with that...no, really.

THREE GIFTS

MARK A RADCLIFFE

époque press

Published by époque press in 2023
www.epoquepress.com

Typeset in Bely Display Regular, Bely Regular
& Bely Italic by Ten Storeys®

British Library Cataloguing-in-Publication Data
A catalogue record for this book is available from
the British Library

ISBN 978-1-7391881-2-2 (Paperback edition)

For Jamie E Auld: 21/06/1958 – 20/02/2020
Who always asked the best questions.

Gift One

1

Francis Broad had negotiated the day of his death, and he was grateful for it. He would die on the 7th of November, aged forty-nine years and eleven months, leaving behind a family he loved, overwhelmed with sadness and a deeply held sense of relief.

At his funeral someone would undoubtedly say, he was very fit for his age, and, forty-nine is nothing really is it? Other things people might say could include, it's not like he was at a high risk of anything was he? He didn't smoke? Did he drink? I don't think so, not so you'd notice, perhaps he drank secretly, because people might imagine or be reassured by an immutable correlation between early death and poor health choices.

One man, a plump chap smelling faintly of tobacco and compost, might head back to the cake that sits on a white tablecloth beside sandwiches and bits of random fruit, secure in the knowledge that exercise and abstinence are ridiculous and overrated, so having a third slice today is winning at life. He won't say that out loud, obviously, that would be inappropriate.

It will be a honey cake. Francis's partner, Victoria, and his fifteen-year-old daughter, Rae, will have made it the night before the funeral, grateful for the task. Honey cake is Francis's favourite. This despite the fact that Rae will say to her mother: why honey cake, he won't be eating it will he? Might as well put some Battenberg out, he hated that for God's sake, and she will cry, again, unable to quite understand why she is so angry with her mum or why Victoria is so angry with her dead husband.

Let's not jump straight to the funeral, though. It is at best macabre and at worst downright rude. Better to scroll back to the night of the 6th of November in New York City.

*   *   *

Francis had arrived back at his hotel in Madison Square Garden at a quarter to eleven at night. He lingered outside for a moment, wondering if he should be thinking something profound, but nothing occurred to him. There was a man standing on the other side of the street singing *God Bless The Child,* badly. His hands, spread out wide as he held the word child on the wrong note for the wrong length of time, his eyes staying tightly closed as if to emphasise just how much he wanted God to do some blessing.

Yes please, thought Francis. *Bless my child,* and he wondered if perhaps Rae, who was about to lose her father, were being punished for the decisions he had made, *but then if I had not made them…*

These thoughts were circular and unremitting, they helped nobody, least of all him so he closed his eyes and let the sounds of the street envelop him. He was completely, ridiculously, almost comically alone, on the wrong side of the planet, in a city he didn't know, waiting to die. He wished he was at home with Victoria and Rae; except he didn't, not really. He wanted to die out of their sight. That, he had decided, was the last act of decency available to him.

He stopped lingering and went inside the hotel lobby where there were people with suitcases coming or going, he didn't care which. He got into an empty lift, pressed the number seven, and wondered if he would speak to anyone ever again. He had waited for this day to come for so long, he had negotiated it and accepted it with all the gratitude he'd gathered over a life that had been laced with gratitude. But he knew that you can feel more than one thing at a time, and he did: sad, scared and lonely.

His room was the same as every bland hotel room in the world. *If there is a heaven,* he thought, *I hope the accommodation is not like this.* He slumped down onto the slightly too firm bed and reasoned that there were five windows of opportunity for death to come for him tomorrow.

The first would be in his sleep, before he woke at 6:45. He liked the idea of a painless death, of deep sleep becoming unconsciously permanent. He had to be up and out of the hotel by 8:30 to catch his flight and he thought that whoever was in charge of ensuring the contract was fulfilled would be saved a lot of trouble if they took him from this miserable little hotel room in the first quarter of the day. Of course, Francis had no idea how much trouble his death was for whoever was in charge of it. It might not need planning at all, it might just be as easy as the clicking of one of eight-billion switches but painlessness appealed nonetheless and so did being found in bed by staff concerned about a late checkout.

The second opportunity was on the way to the airport. He could get mugged, be involved in a fatal car crash, have a cardiac arrest, or, for all he knew, spontaneously combust. He thought about how all of those threats had been available to him every day of his life up to now and for the most part he had never given them a moment's thought. Now, where he had always seen what was essentially a short commute he saw a menu of potential risk; busy roads, falling masonry, disappointed men bearing arms. If he had thought like this earlier in his life he would never have left the house.

The third was whilst he was at the airport waiting to board, wandering through the shops, drinking coffee. He could choke on a muffin, have a heart attack, he could be overcome by perfume in Duty Free. He could just curl up in a ball like a frightened child and sob until the universe took pity on him and turned him off.

The fourth opportunity was on the flight. This felt both the most likely and the most unsettling. Whilst it was possible that he could have a heart attack half-way across the Atlantic and die in the air, he worried about a plane crash because he would take a lot of people with him. *It's not all about me,* he told himself, although he couldn't help but think, *well actually, today it is all about me.*

Taking into account the time difference, he was due to land at 11:50pm on the 7th November, the fifth and final option would involve him dying in his seat as other passengers filed past him; alone on an empty plane, a tired stewardess trying to rouse him. He hoped it wouldn't come to this. He didn't want to die in England, he wanted to die as far away from his family as possible. That was why he had come to New York in the first place.

'Hope you have had a good trip. You'd better have bought me something interesting dad, not a plush King Kong or a T-shirt with the Statue of Liberty on it.' Thoughts of his demise were broken by the message from Rae.

'I'll return the giant monkey immediately,' he texted back.

He had bought her a Velvet Underground T-shirt, a set of guitar plectrums, a tuner and a random pair of dungarees from a flea market in the West Village. He had bought Victoria a silver bracelet and had wrapped all the presents up and written their names on them so when they were given his personal belongings, after the event, they would know whose was whose.

'Have a safe journey, I've been baking up a treat for you.' Victoria texted.

He tried to imagine Victoria with someone else after he had gone. Perhaps a widower to go to the theatre with, although she had friends for that sort of thing. Then he thought of what she would say about him to her friends, to their daughter, to herself. Will there ever be anyone for her to turn to in the dark and say quietly, yes I loved him, but he did something, something I can never understand, or quite forgive.

Francis got up from the bed and sat down at the small desk under the window and took out some writing paper and a pen. If it was true that you lived on in the hearts and lives of those who loved you, then he needed to tell Victoria a secret, something that he could not have told her before.

Dear Vic,
We just finished texting and you said, safe journey, I don't think it will be, and I think I need to tell you why. I think I need to tell you everything now…

Much later he lay back down on the bed and waited for his eyes to close. He slept fitfully, and each time he woke he wondered if this was death coming early. That and *What will my daughter be like when she is eighteen, twenty-five or thirty?*

When morning came he was a little disappointed that he hadn't gone in his sleep after all, the first window of opportunity had been missed and so he quickly packed, posted his letter to Victoria, checked out of the hotel and got into one of the many yellow taxis that flooded the streets outside.

On the way to the airport the driver told him he hoped to visit England one day.

'If you do, go to the coast,' said Francis, for no reason other than that when he thought of England he thought of the sea.

After that brief exchange they sat in silence and Francis stared out of the window looking for potential hazards: a collapsing bridge, snipers near the intersection, and at one point as they overtook a truck that sounded like thunder, he looked to the skies to see if he might be struck by lightning.

When they arrived at JFK he gave the man a big tip and shook his hand. He wasn't sure why, but perhaps he was congratulating him on not being caught up in his story. Or perhaps he just needed to touch human skin one more time.

After he had checked in, he sat and drank a cup of coffee, and then another. Usually he would go to the duty-free and do what Victoria and Rae had christened the airport challenge, a shopping game that consisted of using up whatever local currency they had left buying stuff to take home, but he wasn't going home. The more he sat, the more time that passed, the more he felt a plane crash was the likely winner of the Francis Broad death lottery, a feeling that grew stronger after it was announced that his flight would be delayed by an hour. He would no longer be landing before the day was over, so it was down to option three or four and he wondered what would happen if he simply just sat where he was and waited. Would death come to him? Find him in the corner, take him quietly away? If he didn't get on the plane he would be saving a lot of innocent people from meeting their death, it seemed a clumsy way to take his life; inelegant really, killing two hundred and fifty innocent people just to call in a debt. Or perhaps the plane was going to be full of people who had signed away their lives, just like him?

Or perhaps he was missing the point, what if his death was his responsibility. Why hadn't he thought of that before? Nobody said Death would be along to do the work for him. Maybe once you had signed up for this, you had to do the work yourself? How the hell do you kill yourself in a New York airport? Insult one of the surly men with guns? Shout something threatening at them and tell them you are armed? Run outside and on to the highway?

He was becoming hysterical and took a deep breath. He decided that it was his responsibility to greet Death with something resembling calm expectation and not chase after it like a bewildered puppy. He needed to calm himself down, to counteract the jitters of the caffeine and so he took out the flash drive with the three songs on it that Rae had written.

'You must not listen to them until you are away from England,' she'd said to him before he left. 'And I want to know how they make you feel, Dad, not what you think about them, not how proud are you that your little girl knows some chords and put them together. You are the only grown up I know who talks about feelings, so talk about feelings please.'

This was his girl who not so long ago had been made still by the world and now she was beginning to move again. He texted Rae, 'been listening to those songs again, am I allowed to have a favourite?' He plugged the drive into his laptop, put on his headphones and listened to his daughter sing.

'What did I do when the world disappeared,
I clung to its edge, let uncertainty clear,
I steadied the ship that rolled on the seas
And rested my head on my father's belief'

My little girl wrote that, he thought. Liking the sea thing. And then: What belief? Was it good to rest her head on it? What did she imagine I believed? I wish she told me; I wish I would have been able to ask.

'Course,' she replied straight away.

'First one, although I can't get the third one out of my head.'

'I like the first one best too. See you soon x'

He texted Victoria, 'flight delayed, don't wait up.'

When it was finally time to board he took his headphones off and folded down the screen, thinking, *the laptop could have exploded. That was a missed opportunity.* He boarded the plane, took his seat and waited.

As the plane took off and everything got louder, he noticed that his breathing was accelerating too, like his body knew it had only so much time to gather oxygen before it couldn't but as the carriage began to level out his breathing calmed and when the cabin crew came along the aisle offering drinks he ordered a whisky and coke, thinking that if he was going to go down in a crash he may as well try to make himself as numb to it as possible.

It was three hours into the flight when the turbulence began. At one point it felt as if the plane had dropped a thousand feet in a heartbeat; one person actually screamed. When it settled again, the screamer shouted out 'sorry' in an American accent and lots of people laughed nervously. The seat belt sign stayed on and the cabin crew said the toilets were being closed and passengers needed to stay in their seats.

The old man sitting next to Francis, who must have been eighty and had not spoken until now, turned to Francis and said, 'When the cabin crew stop smiling and look scared, that's the time to worry.'

'How are they looking?' Francis asked.

'Terrified.'

It was then the lights went out and the oxygen masks came down. Francis glanced at the old man, who was sitting perfectly still, not reaching for the mask, he seemed to have his eyes closed and was smiling.

'You don't seem afraid?' said Francis.

'I'm eighty six.'

'You might want to put the mask on anyway, if only to stop the cabin crew from worrying?'

The old man nodded, slowly reached up and pulled the mask down and put it on. Francis did the same. He could now only hear his own breathing and he realised that people with masks on can't scream. He found himself thinking of the safety talk and smiling. *When do we die?* he wondered. *On impact? Will the plane disintegrate? Will we sink to the bottom of the ocean?* He hoped it was on impact, he didn't want to die trapped hundreds of feet under water in a steel tube. That thought filled him with cold terror.

'We have engine difficulty,' the captain announced loudly.

No pleasantries, no predictions. 'And weather difficulties.'

There was a sudden loud bang. Something had struck the plane and the air was sucked out of the cabin. The screaming started again as the plane began to dive and Francis lifted his hand, like a child in a classroom offering an answer to a question. Ridiculous, he knew, but he wanted to say one last thing. Even though it was not profound, significant or audible. 'This is it, I think,' he said.

The old man could not have heard him, but Francis saw him smile. *Maybe he has made the same deal as me, he thought, although at eighty-six he did better than I did.'*

The plane engines were screaming through the hole in the cabin and Francis closed his eyes and thought of Rae. *What would she look like when she turned twenty-five?* and he mouthed silently, *she will be twenty-five.* Then the plane levelled out and seemed to slow down. It was cold, very cold, but quieter, and two of the cabin crew were standing up.

The pilot came on: 'Ladies and gentlemen, we are now flying at a low altitude. This is because an engine part detached and pierced the cabin. The cabin decompression meant we lost our oxygen, but we can breathe at this height. We are now diverting to Reykjavik to land.'

There was half hearted clapping, it stopped quickly, as people realised that they were still twenty thousand feet in the air, stuck in a metal tube with a big hole in the side. Francis wondered if anyone had been sitting where the ejected piece had punctured the plane. He wondered why it had not hit the cabin where he was sitting. If that had killed him, then everyone else could have lived.

'Perhaps we will not be able to land?' Francis said to the old man.

'Perhaps we won't get to Iceland?' replied the man as he turned the oxygen mask over in his hands.

They flew for one hour and forty-five minutes listening to broken metal creak in the wind, clinging to their seats like children on a roller coaster. When they saw some lights on the ground and the pilot said, 'Ladies and gentlemen, that on your left is Iceland,' some people cheered.

'We are now going to land and it will be a bumpy one,' the pilot's voice came back over the speakers, 'so please assume the brace position when instructed, stay in your seats until told otherwise, and follow the instructions of the cabin crew.' He didn't say *try to land*, which Francis thought was admirably confident.

The noise of the approach was deafening and the plane moved from side to side like a drunk dancing. *Better than drowning*, Francis thought, *It will be quick*. He felt the plane touch the ground, heard the squealing tyres desperately trying to slow down. The plane twisted sideways and swung round, slowly at first, before it accelerated and turned a full circle. He imagined it hitting something or tripping its giant self over, or simply falling off the edge of the world because it wasn't a plane anymore, it was just a mass of clumsy metal full of frightened people. But instead, it began rolling backwards, slowing all the time.

As soon as the plane was still, the cabin crew jumped from their seats, opened the doors, and pulled the emergency slides. 'Rows one to ten, now!' Francis remembered he was in row seven and stood up. He waited for the old man, who remained seated.

'Can I help you?' Francis said quietly.

The old man nodded. 'It would appear I am not done yet?'

He stood up slowly and Francis helped him towards the exit. People were streaming down the long rubber slides to be greeted at the bottom by staff who were ushering them away. When Francis's turn came, he nodded at the stewardess and said, 'Thank you,' as if he were getting off in London having slept the whole trip. He let the old man go first and then followed him down the slide. When he reached the bottom he turned to a man in a bright yellow jacket, who was ushering him toward the terminal, and asked him what time it was.

'Just gone midnight, now come on, get moving towards the terminal.'

Francis was still alive. He had not met the terms of his contract.

'How long were we up there?'

'Long enough, now move.'

'It's tomorrow,' Francis said.

'It is.'

'Where is it still today?' Bewildered now and very afraid.

'Where you have just come from sir but by the time you get back there it will be tomorrow there too. Please, follow these people and get inside. You are safe now.'

Nobody had ever been less reassured by those words than Francis was then. His confusion was slowly replaced by anger, He was furious with the pilot for saving his life when it was not his to be saved. *Bastard,* he thought, *what happens now?*

Inside the terminal he sat alone with a blanket wrapped around his shoulders, drinking coffee and staring out the window. A nurse approached him.

'How are you feeling?'

'Confused.'

'Do you have any injuries? Any pain?'

He shook his head. She waited for him to speak but he didn't say anything, and so she moved on. He texted Victoria and Rae. 'I'm in Iceland. Plane diverted, bit of a problem. I'm all right.' A woman with too much foundation on and a man with heavy jowls and anxious eyes, came to see him. They told him that arrangements were being made for passengers to stay in a nearby hotel whilst a replacement plane was arranged.

'Do you understand?' The man asked.

Francis nodded and looked down at his phone. He texted home again: 'all ok there?' *Why on earth am I asking them that?* he thought as he stared at the screen waiting for a reply. Then he thought, *fuck it,* and phoned them.

'Are you alright?' Victoria said as soon as she answered.

'Yes, are you? Is Rae?'

'Yes of course, we're fine; what happened?'

'An engine blew up or something, they thought we would crash, but we didn't.'

'Oh my god, are you sure you are ok, are you hurt?

'I'm fine, a bit shocked, but I'm fine…'

'I have the radio on; it's on the news. Bloody hell Francis.'

'Yeah' he said. 'Bloody hell.'

He had survived the 7th of November, which made a mockery of every thought and feeling he'd had for the last six months. His problem, as he saw it now, was a simple one; if he'd not met his part of the contract, would he still receive what he had so willingly signed away the rest of his life for?

2

When Francis was born, the doctor told his mother that he was very ill and that she should prepare herself for the worst. His mother was an anxious, perennially lonely woman named Rose who had wanted a child more than she believed any woman had wanted one before and she did not know how you were supposed to prepare yourself for the loss of your baby. She thought the doctor must have been mistaken with his advice and she immediately wanted to ask for a second opinion, for someone else to take a look at her constantly screaming new-born. However, it was the 1970s and demanding that cleverer doctors be called upon was not an option for her. Praying was, and so was saying things like; 'He will not die. God would not have given him to me only to take him away again. God is not cruel.'

Rose was considered quite old for a mother, being three months away from her thirty-eighth birthday, and deep down she still believed herself to be a virgin. She was a short, slightly plump woman with grey darting eyes, and the accumulated sense of always feeling like the odd one out had drawn fear onto her face. It was that fear which people saw first when they looked at her. She had been put into foster care by her widowed mother at the age of six, only to be retrieved by her, a stepfather and a baby sister called Ruby, when she was eleven. She did a lot of childcare by way of thanks and worked hard at being useful but she never quite banished the belief that she would be disposable again if the house ever felt too small. It was a feeling she vowed never to pass on to her own child should she ever manage to have one.

Francis's father, Percy, was a big, recurrently absent man who liked to drink and had, in his youth, been considered moderately clever and passably handsome; he retained the slightly inflated confidence that those limited gifts had bestowed. He was something of a faded womaniser, seventeen years older than Rose, with thin red veins showing through his cheeks and exhausted, damp eyes. He almost verified Rose's claims of innocence by openly doubting that he was the baby's father. 'Are you sure it's mine, because believe me that wasn't sex,' he had said the day she had told him she was pregnant. She burst into tears and screamed, 'I have never been touched by another man…how could you even say that?'

Percy was unconvinced. There had been touching, yes, and something akin to intimacy, but his third hand Ford Prefect 100E was a small car with unmovable seats, and he had a bad back. He had offered to drive Rose home at closing time, even though it was out of his way and he had taken the scenic route, along the coast road, where he had stopped near enough to the sea to hear the waves and the wind. Then he put his large, cigarette-stained hand on her knee.

'I'm sorry, I don't know what to do,' Rose had whispered, longing for 'knowing' to not matter.

'Just do what comes naturally,' Percy had replied working hard not to sigh.

None of this comes naturally, thought Rose, along with, why do you still have your coat on?, and, *where did I put my other glove?*

She went straight to bed when she got home, and when she got undressed she noticed her tights were ripped so she hid them at the bottom of her chest of drawers so she wouldn't see them in the morning.

'We didn't actually do it, not properly. Not really,' Rose told her disapproving sister a few weeks later after finding out she was pregnant.

'You have to marry him,' said her sister, a respectable woman married to a bank clerk, who aspired to home ownership and feared that any association with a *fallen woman* could affect her husband's career prospects.

'He hasn't asked me.'

'The bastard,' said her sister, who was called Ruby but wished she wasn't because she thought it made her sound like a barmaid, even though she actually worked part time in a shoe shop and had been one of the first people she knew to own Tupperware.

But Rose's path to the maternity ward didn't matter remotely after the doctor had delivered his verdict.

'He has the wrong sort of blood,' he'd said, or at least that is what she heard.

'Change it,' Rose told him, but he shook his head.

'If only it were that easy,' he mumbled.

Francis was in the intensive care unit, yet Rose could still hear him from the ward she was recovering on. A rhythmic scream, as if the new-born breathed in fire and expelled it as loudly as he could on the fourth beat of every burning bar. The new mothers, who shared the ward with her, held their own children closer and, out of pity or shame or superstition, tried not to look at her. Rose listened to Francis, waiting for him to stop screaming and be brought to her, she was too afraid to sleep, in case it was only her listening that was keeping him alive, she swore a thousand times that once he was, she would never let him go. After four days of listening, Rose was told she should go home.

Back at the house Rose sat in the kitchen, trying to make sense of what was happening whilst making silent deals with God. *I'll never ask for anything else,* she begged, *just let him live.* She shared a council house with Percy and her widowed stepfather in a village called Birchington. They lived beside a field and on a main road. It had three bedrooms and she had painted the smallest white for when she brought her baby home.

Percy stayed out of the house until closing time and when he came home he crept up the stairs to a bedroom that Rose did not even visit. He was usually drunk and slept late. By the time he was awake the next day Rose had gone back to the hospital.

Her stepfather never spoke to Percy. He was a short, stocky man who had spent the last thirty years loading crates of fruit into a lorry and unloading it at various shops in Kent. There was always fruit in the house, sometimes of a type that Rose couldn't identify. He knew that there were no words to be said, so instead he would occasionally leave a cup of tea for her on the Formica table, where it would be left to go cold.

'What if he doesn't come home dad?' she said distractedly.

'He will,' he said, 'I know he will.'

Rose sat outside the ward where her son still screamed. Four days after she had been discharged, on a gloomy overcast Wednesday, she sensed the screaming had become less frequent, quieter, and she wondered if that was because there was less fight or less life left in the child, she concentrated with all of her might on the sound he made. *It is life,* she decided, *I will him to scream.*

Late in the afternoon Percy arrived and announced that he had registered the birth and named the child Francis, despite the fact that he and Rose had agreed that if they had a boy, he would be called Michael. He smelt of beer and she felt a rush of contempt for him then that would never leave her.

It took two more days for the screaming to stop, but stop it did. Rose gripped her hands together so tightly that her nails broke the skin and she stared at the entrance to the ward and begged her God to let her son be alive. Before she had come to the hospital that day she had watched her father limp off to work, he was old now, waiting to retire, his back hurt, his knees hurt, take him, take my father not my son, she had thought and then felt instantly ashamed, not least for imagining that God ran a part-exchange franchise and that someone like her would be allowed to shop there, but also because wishing someone else's life away was wicked, and she was afraid God might punish her for that. Then she thought, take my son's father, and she didn't feel ashamed for that; rather she thought, *Percy should offer that sacrifice himself, that is what fathers should do.*

When the Ward Sister came out, Rose saw something approaching hope in her expression.

'He appears to have turned a corner,' she said. 'He appears settled, the doctors say he is improving, they say the worst is over. He wants to live,'

Rose thanked the Sister and she thanked her God, choosing not to dwell on how the wrong blood could so quickly become the right blood and as she made her way to see her baby she set about thanking every person she saw between the entrance to the ward and the tiny cot her baby lay in. Part of her continued to thank the world every day for the rest of her life and in keeping with the private bargaining she had done with her God as she had waited, never asked the world for anything again.

When she finally stepped into the ward Rose saw a sleeping baby who had sneaked through a crack in the universe to get to her. He was not red now, not angry, not in pain, and Rose was allowed to stroke his hair and slip her finger into his small perfect hands. 'I will keep you safe,' she whispered to the yellow bundle of exhausted flesh. It was her job to keep him alive now, to protect him and guard against any future assault. Rose had purpose and she planned to build her whole life around it.

When she was told that she had to leave, she went home and gave the news to her father, who grinned and said, 'I told you, see, I told you.' Then she went to the telephone box on the corner of the street and called her sister, who said in a flat tone, 'well that's good news. At least you can relax now.' Back at the house she sat at the kitchen table and sipped at the cup of steaming tea her father had made for her. Then she wondered where Percy was.

Percy came home two hours later. He still smelt of beer and when he cried, she couldn't tell if it was the sentimental tears of the drunk or the only expression available to the emotionally illiterate plumber who had been the first and only man she had kissed. He proposed to her that evening and she wondered if a proposal from a man who smelt of beer still counted, but she said yes anyway. thinking that given the fragile hold her son had on the earth, she must never do anything that might even slightly unsettle the natural order or expectation of things. And besides, she had promised to make sacrifices; perhaps this was the first.

They married in the local registry office four months later and not many people came because not many people considered it a celebration. Percy's best man was one of his drinking friends, a man called Bill, whom Rose had never met. He began his speech by saying he was not accustomed to public speaking and then spent several minutes proving it.

'This is a confusing state of affairs,' he said, in a cigarette-coated monotone. 'Not least because the honeymoon came before the wedding.' Right on cue Francis started crying, to helpfully fill the space where nobody laughed.

The reception was held in what was commonly known as the children's room at Percy's favourite pub. It was a drab square room with a portrait of Winston Churchill on the wall and flocked wallpaper that had been randomly scratched off by bored, abandoned kids. Rose wondered if perhaps this was respectability calling, but the idea left her when Percy came out of the gents with a wet patch visible on the front of his trousers. Ruby, who had been the maid of honour whispered, 'You shouldn't have done this you know. People will still think of your son as a bastard.'

'Not near me they won't,' said Rose firmly. 'The boy needs a father, doesn't he?' Her question, that began as rhetorical, turned into something like resignation halfway through.

Within ten minutes of the cake being cut, Percy had

wandered into the bar next door and was watching a horse race on the television. Rose left the pub before it was dark, taking her son home.

'I need to feed him and get him to bed,' she'd said, and nobody argued because that was indeed what mums had to do with babies.

Francis, who hadn't stopped crying since the honeymoon joke, appeared relieved by the clear dusk air. He didn't like the cigarette smoke and like his mum, he didn't seem terribly keen on the smell of beer either.

3

'Tell me about when I was a baby,' asked the six-year-old Francis.

'You were beautiful. Hard to believe now, I know.'

'No, when I was born and I nearly died.' Francis poked his mother in the fleshy part of her arm. They were sitting on the sofa, Grandad was asleep in his chair. He had retired nearly a year earlier and had been resting ever since. Francis thought he was shrinking. When he was little, Grandad would play with him. That seemed beyond him now. He didn't seem able to bend anymore. And there was no fruit now, sometimes Francis missed bananas and apples. He didn't have a clear sense that they were poor but he knew there were limits on what was available, sometimes that included food.

Tomorrow's World was on the television, it was promising jet packs and protein pills instead of food. Dinner had been eaten, Francis was still hungry nonetheless.

'They said you had the wrong blood,' she said dramatically.

'What does that even mean,' said Francis, thrilled and appalled in equal measure. 'Like I was an alien?' He was tall for his age, full of awkward energy, looking at the world with wide, hungry eyes.

'I don't know son, I'm not a doctor. I think it is because I have a rare blood group.'

'What's a blood group?'

'Like a flavour. There are several different flavours, I think. Some of them are common, some of them are rare; they don't all mix with each other.'

'But why would my blood be wrong?'

'I think it was just different, not wrong.'

'So, your blood and my blood was like mixing two flavours that don't go together?

'Yes, like Strawberry and Cauliflower.' Rose put her arm around him. 'You're the cauliflower.'

'Like banana and hedgehog, and you are the hedgehog,' Francis giggled.

'When you were ill, I prayed and I hoped…and I believed deep down that you would be all right.'

It was this that Francis liked the most, that his mum had believed in him even before she knew him and that believing really hard, so hard that it makes your eyes close tightly shut and your veins stand out, made things happen, important things.

'And what did Grandad do?'

'He believed too son.'

They cuddled into each other and looked at Grandad asleep in his chair with his mouth open.

'How old is Grandad?' Francis whispered.

'Sixty-six.'

'That is very old,' gasped Francis.

'It looks it, doesn't it,' Rose said quietly.

'Do you worry about him?' Francis asked.

'Worry about what?'

'About him falling over and not being able to get up again.'

'Well…I do now.'

'Don't worry,' Francis said seriously. 'If he falls, I will catch him.'

Rose kissed him on the top of his head and said, 'If he falls you'll get out of the way. I don't want you being crushed by a falling grandad.'

Falling happened sometimes. Birthdays and New Year's Eve, for example, when drink had been taken, and they would have to get one of the neighbours round to help him back up again. But falling wasn't the main problem. Forgetting, was the main problem and increasingly, accidentally weeing before he could get to the toilet.

'What about dad, what did dad do?'

Rose laughed, 'he waited.'

'Down the pub?'

'Down the pub…'

Percy had finally given up on the pretence of family life and had left the three-bedroom council house just before Francis had turned four. He had practiced leaving before. Some of those departures had been drunken, some had been sulky, and some had been because following one of his previous exits, he had begun renting a bedsit four miles away in a small town called Cliftonville, and he vaguely felt that he should try to get his money's worth from it. Francis preferred it when his father was somewhere else, not because he particularly disliked him, he had never really spent enough time with him to form a clear view, but because all the coming and going was quite unsettling for his mother, and when she was unsettled, it tended to leak out all over Francis's world.

After the front door had slammed on Percy's final departure, Francis went into the kitchen where his mum was sitting at the small Formica table with her head in her hands. He thought about offering her his talking Action Man, but it only said three things, the most common of which was 'Action Man patrol, fall in,' which didn't seem likely to help, and so he patted her shoulder and said, 'Will he come back?'

'I don't think so son, not this time.' said Rose, who had pink bags under her eyes.

And Francis said, 'I hope not.'

Rose looked surprised. 'Why do you say that?'

'He's not really here when he is here, and he makes you sad.'

Rose put her arms round him. 'Little boys are supposed to have fathers.'

'I like it best when he isn't here though. There is more room, less shouting. Grandad doesn't talk when Daddy is here.'

Rose began to laugh and cry at the same time. 'We're all right, aren't we, son?'

And Francis was all right, he had never really known what a dad was for anyway and normal is whatever it is you become used to. He didn't covet other people's lives or dads and when they visited Aunt Ruby's house it always seemed so noisy to him and he liked quiet best. As far as Francis was concerned, there was no need for the large and noisy presence of a dad stomping around the house occasionally shouting, although he was sure that all dads couldn't have been like that. He saw some of the children at school being picked up by their dads and they would be wrapped up in cuddles and tickles and given bags of sweets. Even if some dads were ok though, Francis wasn't interested because he had his mum and she was kind and good and they made each other laugh even when they weren't supposed to, like when they would hide from the insurance man who came round on a Tuesday evening.

'Do you think he knows we are here?' Francis asked the first time he had been told to lay down on the floor until the man at the door had gone away.

'Shh. Probably, shh,' Rose was pressed tight against the wall. Francis thought she looked like a spy. He pressed himself against the floor beside the sofa.

'Why don't you tell him you will pay him next week?' he whispered.

'I told him that last week.'

'Mum,' he said in a stage whisper, 'I think I could probably get right underneath the sofa if we had to do really good hiding.'

'Good boy, well done, now shh.'

Any lingering fear Rose may have had that Francis would be sickly following his hesitant entry into the world was eliminated by his endless energy. Francis ran around like he was trying to catch the sky, much to the irritation of Grandad, who was increasingly prone to weeing on the floor on his slow, shuffling walk to the toilet.

'Can't you sit still?' He would bark and Francis would think him ridiculous. *Why would I sit still? It looks awful.*

But Francis started to play outdoors whenever he could, escaping the smell of his grandads' wee and only going back in reluctantly when it was dark.

Francis was seven when the divorce was finalised and he would have chosen to ignore it, and just get on with things as they were if he had been allowed. He didn't really mind being the boy who didn't have a father but he was forced to go out on fortnightly trips with his dad which would usually involve driving to a pub, where Francis was allowed to sit behind the steering wheel of his father's Ford Anglia and pretend to drive it, while Percy attended to important business inside. After one of these trips Rose was waiting for them on the kerbside outside the house and she had said to Percy that there was no point in him taking the boy out if he was going to keep him locked in a car for hours whilst he got drunk. On the next trip Percy decided to surprise his son, and perhaps himself, by taking him to the beach.

It was a sunny, breezy early summer's day, and the long yellow sand of Margate was laced with families sitting in deck chairs and children running to and from the water's edge with buckets. The men rolled their trousers up and took off their jackets, revealing long-sleeved shirts and braces. Their wives all wore summer dresses that exposed red arms and strong calves and they busied themselves protecting the long-prepared picnic of fish-paste sandwiches from the sand. Unlike these other families it was clear that their trip had just been an afterthought; there was no picnic, no deckchairs and unlike the other children, no swimming costumes.

'It's fine,' his father said. 'Your pants are just the same as swimming trunks. Nobody will know the difference.'

Other children always knew the difference though.

'Are they your pants?' a boy said when Francis had asked to look at the crabs, he'd collected in his plastic bucket.

'Not really,' said Francis, caught between a truth and a lie.

The other boy shrugged. 'I caught them all on my own. I'm going to kill them.'

'Why?' asked Francis.

The boy looked at Francis as if he were an idiot and shrugged again. 'Because I caught them.'

Francis liked the beach, particularly the point where the sea met the sand, like a hesitant guest bearing the promise of a gift. He would run into the water until it was up to his belly button, then, for no reason, become scared of falling over and never standing up again. So, he would turn and run back toward his father who, like all the other men, had rolled his trousers up, but like nobody else, had kept his coat on and had a face as red as the plastic bucket with the crabs in. As soon as Francis was back on the beach the fear left him and the sight of his father made him feel something else, something he couldn't name but it might have been embarrassment, so he would turn and run back into the water, up to his middle again. He did this over and over, running in and out of the sea, occasionally throwing himself down when knee deep and pulling himself along by his hands on the bottom, pretending to be swimming, pretending to be brave.

As he ran back into the sea for the ninth or tenth time he lifted his head to look out beyond the harbour and something caught his eye. It was a swimmer wearing a red swim hat, a long way out beyond everyone else, where the sea changed colour and somehow looked flatter. He stared, watching the thin, slow, looping arms cartwheel across the horizon.

'Is that person ok?' he asked his father.

'I'm sure they are,' said his father, without raising his eyes from his paper. 'Have you had enough now?'

'Five more minutes please?'

His father sighed and looked at his watch. 'Alright,' he said.

Francis raced back down the beach and plunged into the shallows, determined to get as wet as five minutes would allow. He began to pull himself along by rotating his arms, like the swimmer out in the deep water but his face went under and he panicked. He quickly stood up, spouting water from his mouth, and glancing up the beach to see if his father would come to help he didn't notice the man walking past him until he saw a shadow on the water.

'Nice stroke don't be scared, the water will hold you.' said the man, very quietly as if sharing a secret.

Francis watched as the man, with a red rubber cap and a pair of goggles dangling from his hand, strode out of the sea and up the beach towards his dad. Francis dragged himself out and followed on behind.

'Looks like there is a bit of a current out there?' Percy said, looking past the man out to where he had been swimming.

'There is. It made me work for it today.'

Francis was panting heavily and slumped down beside his dad.

'Your boy?' The swimmer asked, looking toward Francis, 'He seems to love the water?'

'This is his first time.' Percy said, with something approaching a hint of pride, and then more quietly, 'I think.'

'Well, have a good day,' the swimmer said as he walked off up the beach.

'You are going to need to learn to swim, young man,' said Percy, as if identifying a need was a significant contribution toward meeting it.

'Can you swim?' Francis asked.

'I can.' his dad said as he looked out past the harbour and not at his son.

'You could teach me?' Francis said.

'We'll see,' Percy replied.

And Francis knew that that meant no, not least because it would have involved his father taking off his car coat.

*   *   *

Percy died of cancer when Francis was eight. He had not taught him to swim. Or how to do anything else. Ironically, his father was around more in the final six months of his life than he had been for the preceding seven and a half years. Francis reflected later that before he had cancer, his dad was absent, irresponsible, volatile, unreliable, and moody. After he was diagnosed, he stopped being most of those things and was mostly scared and lonely. The cancer began in Percy's bladder, moved quickly to his liver, took up squatting rights in his lungs and spread outward like a bush fire. He carried on living in his bedsit for as long as he could, but he increasingly came to his old family house for an uneaten dinner and awkward company.

When Percy stayed late into the evening, and they all sat and watched television, the tiny living room seemed full of decaying male flesh. Francis would sit on the sofa with his mother, imagining the smell of his father rotting away on the inside trying to overcome the constant aroma of urine that emanated from Grandad. The house, which was small to start with, had shrunk around the men, pressing inward, amplifying their silent disdain for each other.

Francis would try to avoid them as much as possible and he would spend as long as he could in the garden playing football against imaginary teams, commentating on himself as he ran past clumps of grass and uncut daisies. When he was too tired to continue, he would go upstairs to his room, where he would lay on his bed and write match reports of the games he had played into an exercise book, and draw pictures of trees or flowers or clouds. When that was done he would stare out the window, trying to guess what tomorrow's weather would be by looking at the sky in the distance and how much the trees were moving in the wind. When it had grown too dark to see the sky properly he would turn to the picture books that he'd borrowed from the library, hard back books that smelt of dust and vinegar and had maps inside of different countries with pictures of the animals that lived there and the trees that grew there. His mother would call him to come down, but he would ignore her and then she would call again, less patient, more insistent. All this whilst his father sat decaying downstairs.

Percy died during the school summer holidays and Francis was not allowed to go to the funeral because his mother didn't believe children should watch bodies be burned. By the time Francis had returned to school, his father had been dead for five weeks and he didn't feel it worth mentioning. He wrote a story though, about a man who had tree bark for skin but who becomes more human on the outside as he gradually begins to putrefy on the inside.

'It was a very good story,' his teacher had said to his mum at parents evening. 'Mind you some of the imagery was quite unsettling.'

'He does have a good imagination. He watches a lot of television. *The Big Match, Banacek, Scooby Doo, Macmillan and Wife*, that's alright, isn't it?' Rose had said, afraid that revealing her son's viewing habits had exposed a shortfall in her parenting.

'Is there anything else I should be aware of that might be affecting him?' replied a slightly confused Mr Matthews.

There was a silence.

'You know his father died in the summer. I did tell the

Headmaster about it.'

'No, no I didn't, I am so very sorry, Mrs Broad.'

'Well, Francis doesn't talk about it much. When I ask him how he feels, he says fine and goes outdoors. He is happier outdoors. But…'

'I will keep an eye on him,' Mr. Matthews said, and noticing instantly that Rose looked frightened, added 'to see that he is ok, not too sad, not isolated, or anything.'

Rose wondered what too sad looked like but, ever respectful, thanked him and asked. 'Is he doing well in his lessons?'

'Yes, yes, very well. He could pass his 11+, assuming this loss doesn't affect him too deeply.'

'I'm sure it won't,' Rose said before standing up and saying 'I won't keep you any longer, thank you for your time'; she almost bowed as she left.

When she got home she didn't mention the story, or Mr. Matthews saying that he would keep an eye on Francis, but she did ask, 'You are ok son, aren't you?'

'Of course I am,' shrugged Francis.

The first sign that he may not have been came a few weeks later. Rose looked in on her son before she went to bed to find him curled up in a ball, fast asleep, clinging on to one of her cardigans. He had wrapped it round his arms, bunching it so that it gathered around his face. She crept over to his bed and tried to gently take the cardigan away, thinking that he would get too hot with pink acrylic wrapped around his head and as she gently pulled, smiling at the thought that perhaps the child found her scent reassuring, Francis gripped tighter. She pulled again and his eyes opened, empty of recognition, full of instinctive rage. 'No!' he shouted loudly and snatched the sleeve of the cardigan away, clenching himself more tightly into a ball, like an animal that wished it had spikes to ward away invaders. Rose stepped away, momentarily scared, and watched the boy go back to sleep.

He slept like that every night from then on, wrapping himself in acrylic simply became a habit for him, and Rose abandoned the cardigan and said nothing for fear that she would embarrass him.

A few weeks later Rose was calling Francis to come downstairs for school and he was ignoring her. After three or four attempts she went to the foot of the stairs to shout more loudly to only find him sitting on the top stair holding on to the banister and staring at her.

'Come on' she said, 'you'll be late.'

'I can't,' he said.

'Can't what?'

'I can't come down the stairs'

'Well, you managed yesterday.'

'But I can't today.'

'Francis, stop messing around,' she said, scared again.

'It's too high, too far. I can't.'

'I'll help you,' said Rose as she walked slowly up the stairs toward him.

Francis looked at his mother and felt safe and ashamed at the same time.

'You hold my hand, and I'll go down on my bottom,' Francis said, 'but not too fast.'

And that is how he got downstairs, every day for six weeks, until finally, reluctantly, Rose took Francis to see the Doctor.

4

Rose had always been prone to bouts of sadness and occasional despair and usually she was not afraid to let those feelings out and into the world. If she was happy, she laughed, if she was angry, she shouted or threw things, and if she was miserable, she cried. She could do all of those on the same day, sometimes the same hour, but sadness was something of a resting position when Francis was small, and her life was such that it was rarely difficult to find something to hang that sadness on. Poverty was key to that. They lived on *Supplementary Benefit*. Rose did not work because she couldn't leave her father alone. Percy had left nothing, certainly not a pension, sometimes, usually the day before benefit day, there was not enough food for them all. Loneliness was a constant for her too: whilst she may not have actually missed her husband, she missed the idea of a one, and perhaps more importantly, she felt different to the other women, because she was a single mother. It was hard to tell if she actually craved companionship, or just convention. Whichever it was, she was riddled with a self-consciousness that she would call shame. All of this was compounded by the fear that gripped her when her son became afraid of the stairs and Rose believed, above all of the things she felt, that she was responsible, she was failing him, and she deserved to feel the way she did.

The family doctor was a kindly stout man called Doctor Gordon. He listened to Rose fill the room with her son's nerves as she called it, which he named anxiety.

'He has experienced quite a lot for a little boy,' Doctor Gordon said, looking at Francis. 'I'm going to suggest you see a colleague of mine, very good at helping childr...young people like yourself, Francis. She comes here for a day a week, a Thursday, is that all right Mrs Broad?'

They came together the following Thursday, straight after school. In the waiting room Francis recognised a girl from his class who, when she saw Francis, went to her father and buried her face into his neck. Francis stared at the carpet, which was grey with faint white spirals; he didn't want to see the girl again, so he began to count the strands of carpet that had been dipped in white. He thought of them as trees in a tiny forest and began to imagine being so small he could walk and hide among them.

'Don't be nervous,' Rose said, as if she were speaking to herself, and Francis felt irritated. When the girl was called he stopped staring at the floor and watched her go into the Doctor's room.

'Do you know her?' asked Rose.

'She goes to my school,' he said quietly.

'I wonder where her mother is?'

'I don't think she has one.' Francis said. 'People don't play with her; she wet herself in assembly.'

'Poor girl,' Rose said, and Francis shrugged because people

didn't play with him either and he hadn't even wet himself.

Doctor Ingrid Connor was a small, thin woman with black hair, kind eyes and slightly too much face powder. She wore a white coat, which made Francis nervous, and a necklace with a large purple stone shaped like a heart. Francis thought she spoke like a newsreader: clipped, clever and knowing. When she asked him a question she tried to smile at the end of it and turned her head slightly as if she were offering a glimpse of her ear for him to speak into. She told them both her name, but she would simply be known to Rose and Francis as the *Lady Doctor*.

'When you are at the top of the stairs, do you ever feel dizzy?' she asked.

'Not really.'

'He is sitting,' interrupted Rose, 'he sits on the top stair, don't you Francis?'

The Doctor looked at Rose and smiled, then she turned her attention back to Francis and waited to see if he had anything to add. He didn't.

'What is it you are afraid of when you are at the top of the stairs?'

Francis tried to think. The obvious thing would be to say falling, but he wasn't sure that was true. When he was up there looking down, he wondered if there might be something bad downstairs waiting for him, like a pool of crocodiles or quicksand.

'Falling.' Rose spoke into the silence, 'I think he is scared of falling, what else is there to be afraid of?'

The Doctor looked at Rose and said, 'Mrs. Broad, how would you feel about sitting outside for a few minutes?'

Rose didn't know what to say. Why couldn't she be there?

She was his mother; it was her duty to be with him. Would this doctor try to take him away? Say that she was a bad mother? Rose could not conceive of anything in the world that was a worse thing to be than a bad mother.

'I can see you love your son very, very much Mrs. Broad. I want to help. There is nothing to worry about, I would just like some time alone with Francis if that is ok with you?'

Rose turned to Francis. 'Do you mind if I sit outside so you can talk to the doctor in private?'

'I don't mind,' Francis said quietly as Rose reddened slightly.

'All right,' she said standing up. 'Don't forget to tell the doctor about the cardigan, the one you hold on to when you sleep.'

Now it was Francis who blushed. He felt his mother was cross with him and he didn't know why, so he felt cross back at her.

'Francis?' Rose said.

'Ok,' he said loudly.

The doctor waited until Rose had gone, then crossed her legs and forced a smile. Francis could see the lines on her face, beneath her makeup, creak into life.

'Do you want to tell me about the cardigan?' she asked.

'It's pink,' Francis shrugged, 'but I'm not sure that matters.' The doctor waited.

'I just found myself holding it when I fell asleep once.'

'Does it feel nice? Does it smell nice?'

It smelt of flowers and his mother. Francis nodded.

'Some people say that smell is the most powerful of the senses.'

'I like my eyes the best,' Francis said.

'I think I like my eyes best too, but I do wonder if that is because I take the other senses too much for granted. Now Francis, can I ask you about your father? Do you miss him?'

'Not really,' Francis said quickly.

'What do you feel when you think about him?'

Francis hesitated for a moment, what did he feel? If he didn't say sad it would make him a bad person, but sad felt wrong. Sad was like the feeling you had when it was the end of summer holidays.

'Why did you say, not really, when I asked if you missed him?'

Francis thought for a moment, 'I think my mum worries about me not having a dad and there isn't anything she can do about it, and if I miss him or something...'

'She might feel bad?'

Francis looked at the floor.

'Did your father live with you?'

'Not really.'

'What does that mean?'

'He left when I was little.'

'And what was that like?'

'They argued. It was quieter.'

'What was it like for you?'

'I said, quieter.'

'Do you remember playing with him or laughing with him?'

'He took me to the beach once, but I'm not sure he liked me very much.'

'Why do you think that?'

'Well, he left, lots of times, and when we were together he always seemed to have somewhere else he needed to be.'

'And then he died. Which is another way of leaving really,

isn't it?' said Doctor Connor.

That seemed a little harsh, thought Francis. *He couldn't help dying. And he probably didn't do it just to get away from me.*

Later, when Francis was sitting outside trying to draw the plastic flowers that sat on the table in the waiting room the doctor spoke with Rose.

'He is a lovely young boy, you must be very proud.'

'I am proud.' Brittle and guarded.

'I think it is hard for one so young to lose their father.' The doctor spoke as if Rose were the patient now, clear and reassuring.

'He wasn't much of a father.'

'Then he lost two fathers perhaps?'

Rose looked confused.

'He lost the dad he knew, the one who took him to the beach once and might have again eventually, and he lost the dad he didn't have, the father other boys have, one he won't get to meet now?'

'I do my best…'

'Oh, Mrs Broad, you are doing wonderfully, this is not about you. He sleeps with your cardigan because you make him feel safe, he smells you on it and he can relax. He wraps himself around it so you can't go anywhere when he is asleep…'

Rose began to cry, 'he knows I won't ever leave him.'

'Of course he does.'

'I can tell him, I can tell him every day…'

'Yes, but I would suggest you show him as well. He needs to feel needed. His father didn't help with that, he made Francis feel…disposable…or like a task. I think he needs to feel he is useful. You might start by giving him jobs to do, like going to the shop for you.'

Mark A Radcliffe

'He is too young...'

'Is he? Is it far? Let him do things around the house. Tell him when he helps.'

'I can do that.'

'Good.'

Rose was sniffling into a handkerchief. 'And the stairs?'

'It will pass.'

'When?'

'When he feels safe. When he is stuck at the top of the stars it is his way of making sure that you can't leave him.'

'He knows I will never desert him...' Rose began to cry again.

The next day, Rose said to Francis, 'when do you think you will be big enough to go to the shop on your own?'

Francis looked confused, 'I am big enough now.'

'Are you? I was wondering, we need milk and if I give you the money could you go and buy some for me?'

'Now?'

'What do you think? I mean I could go, but I have to make dinner and my ankle is sore and...' she couldn't think of anything else to make up, she was afraid that she was doing something wrong, she was afraid of the road, she was afraid that in the hundred-yard walk to the local shop something or someone would swoop in and steal her boy.

'I can do that,' Francis said, excited, nervous, like he was going on a mission.

'Make sure you get the change and be very careful crossing the road.'

He was not the only eight-year-old going to the local shop but when he got back that first time he felt he had grown. He began to do other things as well. He would cut potatoes into chips without losing any fingers. He offered to open the door

42

to the insurance man and say that Rose was out, but Rose said no to this for fear the insurance man would contact social services. He even started making tea in the mornings for his mother.

'Leave it in the pot a bit longer please, it has to brew,' she would say every day but drank it anyway.

When they went back to see the lady doctor two months later, Rose said, 'he has become a little man.' She meant it as a compliment, a boast even, and was surprised the Doctor didn't smile.

'I can come down the stairs now. I do it on my bottom, but I can do it.' Francis said it in as matter-of-fact way as he could. He felt proud and he thought the lady doctor seemed proud of him as well.

'What else has changed?' asked Doctor Connor. She was looking at the boy and Rose bit her lip.

'I go to the shop. I try to help. It is hard for mum. I try to look after her.'

Rose looked embarrassed and then cross, and Francis didn't know what he had said wrong. Rose believed a difficult life should be hidden.

'It is nice that you want to help, Francis' said Doctor Connor.

'He does help.' Rose reached out and touched his shoulder. 'We help each other, don't we son.'

'Yeah, we do.'

Helping was good, it felt grown up, and it made things better, not just for his mum but for himself too, he could even come down the stairs now. Francis thought that the lady doctor was very clever.

'It is my job to look after my mum,' he said, decisively and he knew then that it always would be.

5

As Francis grew he became more aware of some of the things he wasn't very good at: stairs, making friends, science, fitting in, making tea. At school he felt like the odd one out and the harder he tried the odder he seemed. It was like he didn't have the same glue as the other boys, the type that bound them together, like the way they dressed – his uniform was always somehow less than everyone else's, his polyester trousers not quite as black, his blazer not quite the right size – or the way they spoke, or the games they played. The other boys could see it when they looked at him and that made him prey.

Despite this Francis tended toward optimism. It was an optimism that appeared naive to his sneering peer group, so he enjoyed the small victories when they came: running fast, being good at football, winning on sports day and getting better at stairs without other people knowing he was rubbish at them in the first place. He didn't always need the cardigan to sleep with either. He still used it sometimes, but there were nights when he felt brave, or tired, and even though Rose would always leave it on his bed, he pushed it to the bottom, careful to never let it slip on to the floor, because that would be rash, and slept near it rather than in it.

In the evenings, after school, Francis would play outdoors, alone, for as long as he could. The council estate they lived on backed on to potato fields and at the age of ten he would run across them with joyous abandon, feeling as though he were getting away from something, even if he didn't know what it was he was getting away from. He would run as fast as he could until he was too puffed out to carry on. Then he would stop, bend over, rest his hands on his knees and laugh, his own victorious celebration.

To the left of his house there was a long hill leading up to more fields and when he ran to the top of it there was nothing to hear there but his own breathing. To the right of his house were more fields leading to a railway line which he had never crossed. Trains, Rose would warn, are dangerous, 'you could fall over on the rails and get run over by a train,' she would say, and he would try to imagine what that would be like and became a little afraid of trains. But boundaries are there to be crossed and on the other side of the railway line was a straight run to the beach. It was not the same beach Percy had taken him too, but rather one that families and tourists didn't bother with. One with pebbles and seaweed and, when the tide was out, a long walk to the sea. It was two miles from Francis' house and one day, without really having decided to, he ran there. Picking his way across the trainline like it was a minefield.

The beach was called Minnis Bay and it was bigger, longer and more expansive than the village itself. It could be sandy or seaweedy depending on what the water had decided to deposit on the land. It could smell of salt or candyfloss, and it could sound like screaming children or weeping gulls or swirling winds depending on what your ears tuned into. Francis came to realise that the sea reorganised itself every day; it could be green, grey or any shade of blue, it could be still like ice, or dance and shout with wild abandon. Sometimes when the waves crashed together it sounded like laughter, other times it could sound frightening or thrilling or indifferent or foreboding. It took Francis a long time to realise that the way the sea sounded was the way he felt. If he'd had a bad day at school, if the other boys had simply not spoken to him, or worse, stood beside him and talked about him; about his uniform or his hair or his weirdness or his shoes, the sea would roar his rage. It spoke to him and after it had, he always felt stronger.

One cold and icy January day, the first time in a week when it had not been raining, Francis had found that somebody at school had drawn breasts on his woodwork apron. He had tried to wash them off in the toilets but the ink, rather like the disdain, was indelible. He did woodwork with his apron inside out to a backdrop of sniggering. On the Friday afternoon of that week he had sat in double maths with a hunched and crumbling teacher called Mr Cook who didn't like him and as far as Francis could tell had no eyes, just bags of flesh gathered in the middle of his face through which he gazed out at the young with utter contempt. Francis hated Maths, the only counting he did during the lesson was of the seconds he was wasting by being there. Mr Cook had pointed at one of his shoes and said, 'you have a hole in your shoe Broad, does your mother know that?' The other kids had sniggered, Francis had blushed. Of course she knew it, that didn't mean she could do anything about it. You can't just mend shoes.

'I'm going for a run,' he said to his mother as soon as he got home.

'What's happened, love?' his mum said as if he were seven.

'School. School happened.'

'Talk to me?' Rose said gently.

'I just want to go for a run mum,' Francis' eyes wereburning, and he knew what he would see when he looked at the water today.

'Dinner at six, ok?' Rose sighed.

He got changed quickly, unsure if his mother would stop him with more pointless questions or if the rain would come and he would be told he had to stay indoors. The plastic clock above the gas fire read 4:45 and he knew he could run to the sea and back and hardly be late at all, especially if he ran fast, and today of all days he needed to run fast.

It began to rain within five minutes of Francis leaving the house and it caught him in the eyes and stung his face as he ran headlong into it. Each time he turned a corner he expected some relief but, the wind couldn't make its mind up as to which way to blow and the rain still lashed at him as he was buffered and pushed sideways, losing the rhythm of his pace. But he kept on running, faster and faster until he saw the sea looming large behind the dusk. It was grey and rearing and wholly without order, which was exactly what he was too.

Breathing hard he stopped, where he always stood, on the concrete promenade that overlooked the sea. He stared down at the waves as they crashed back from the promenade wall and he thought about running straight back home, faster, harder, punching himself from the inside, but he knew that would not be enough and he didn't want to go home anyway.

Rubbing the rain from his face he looked out over the thick shades of grey and saw a red dot in the water, moving up and down with the waves. At first he doubted himself, it couldn't be a person could it, nobody would swim in this; perhaps someone might have fallen from a boat or been swept off the promenade and dragged out into the freezing wild water.

Francis looked along the promenade for a grown up but there was nobody around; no lifeboats, no coastguards, no dog walkers, nobody stupid enough to be out in this weather. Further along the promenade was a phone box and he wondered if he should run there and call the coastguard and tell them that someone was in trouble, that it wasn't a hoax, that this was real and that of course he was happy to give them his name and address, but the longer he looked at the swimmer, the less anxious he became.

The red dot was now moving slowly towards the slipway, about three hundred yards from where Francis was standing. Their stroke steady and unchanging, no sign of distress, so, Francis ran down to where the waves came crashing into the wall, sending a shower of spray up over him, and he stood transfixed by the bobbing red hat that was making its way toward him. As the waves hit the wall they caused a backwash around the slipway and the swimmer stopped just short of it, treading water, trying to gauge the rhythm of the swell. As far as Francis could tell, there was no rhythm to it and he began to worry again, thinking he had lost the opportunity to call for help. But the swimmer edged forward slowly, getting close twice only to change their mind and swim away again. On the third attempt the swimmer quickly launched themselves forward from fifteen yards out, coming at an angle that cut across the waves. They caught a swell which lifted them up and set them down feet first onto the concrete. The swimmer quickly ran up the slipway and onto the promenade where Francis was standing.

'Don't stand too close to the edge young man,' said the swimmer as he took off his hat and goggles and reached down to his rucksack to pull out a large fluffy towel, which he rubbed vigorously across his head of grey flecked hair. 'And thank you for keeping an eye on me.'

Francis knew that he should never talk to strangers but decided that today he would make an exception, in part because the man seemed familiar.

'That looked really scary.'

'Yeah, I wouldn't recommend it.'

'Do you do this a lot?'

'Swim? Yes.'

'Have I seen you before.'

'You might have done, I'm down here a lot,' said the man, who had finished towelling his head and was now looking directly at Francis whilst quickly drying his upper body and arms. 'I think I have seen you before. You look older than the first time, but I have noticed you running down here a lot.'

That made Francis nervous, and he instinctively took a step back.

The man smiled and started drying his legs. 'People who come to the sea alone like to imagine they are invisible,' he smiled, 'but nobody ever is.'

'I didn't know whether I should have called for help.'

'Why didn't you?'

'Should I have?'

'Do you always answer a question with a question?'

'Were you in danger?'

The man dropped his towel to the floor and pulled out a long-sleeved top from his bag which he pulled on, followed by another and then a thick woollen jumper.

'You were absolutely right to think about calling for help but right to wait for a few minutes to see if I knew what I was doing. Well done.'

Francis blushed, he wasn't used to be told he had done something well. Particularly by a man, or on reflection, anyone other than his mum.

'And you did know what you were doing?'

'People who swim in conditions like this are idiots, but I have been an idiot for a very long time so…if you'll excuse me, I need to get these swimming trunks off and I suspect you need to get home for tea?'

Francis looked at his watch, it was six thirty and he knew his mum would be cross if he was too late, and she would certainly not be calmed if he told her he got distracted talking to a man who was getting dressed in the rain.

'Yes, I'm late,' said Francis and then he turned away and started to run home.

6

If Rose had been invited to share an anecdote about her life, unlikely because there were not many people who listened when Rose spoke, it would not reflect the drama and humiliation that accompanied poverty but rather it would end in a small triumph. Rose's version of herself was always winning, albeit in the smallest of ways.

When the cancer came to her, she may have felt terrified and defeated, she may have cursed her dead husband for leaving the disease in the house for her to catch, and she might have sobbed every night until she could barely breathe and worried herself even sicker over what would happen to her twelve-year-old son. But it is also possible that Rose decided to pray really hard and believe that her God would protect her, because despite appearances and most of the superficial evidence, Rose believed she was one of life's winners. Or she had been until now.

As her son grew, her victories tended to gather around him. She recognised him to be a sensitive child and blamed herself for this, mainly because blaming herself for things came naturally to her. He was healthy and won races on sports day, he did alright at school, he didn't get into trouble, and he was helpful, which was a good quality to have, something to be encouraged.

Yes, he had forgotten how to come down the stairs, even though there were only thirteen of them, but he had overcome the fear, at first by coming down on his bottom, then by standing and coming down sideways with both hands holding the banister, and then eventually, calling her and saying 'look mum' as he walked, head high and facing out in front rather than down. touching down at the end and celebrating like he had scored the winning goal in the Cup Final.

He still slept with his bedroom door open though, and Rose would rush to him two or three times a week to ease him from bad dreams that saw him pulled by his feet into quicksand or thrown into a deep dark well or simply locked into a small room with white walls and no door. He would slowly describe the dreams to her, embarrassed that such simple fears should make him scream, adding something at the end to make his terror seem more reasonable:

'The quicksand filled my throat, I began to choke,' he would say, or 'the room was a thousand feet high and at the end, I think the walls began to move toward me, to crush me.'

'Shh,' she would say, 'it's just a dream,' and he would reach out toward the old cardigan at the foot of the bed, and she would hand it to him and sit until his face softened into a less painful sleep.

So no, it wasn't what her cancer might do to her that frightened Rose, it was what her absence would do to her son. She had sworn to protect him when he was a screaming baby and he still needed protecting now; deserting him, letting him down, made her feel wicked.

'Guess who did it,' Francis said at the start of *Murder On The Orient Express,* as they settled down to watch it a week after Rose had first received the news from her doctor.

'Everybody,' Rose said flatly.

'Oh come on mum,' Francis chided. 'Join in.'

'I am joining in.'

'No you're not. What's the matter?'

'Nothing is the matter. I'm telling you, everybody did it.'

'What the train driver did it, Poirot did it, that woman in the floppy hat did it…'

'Well not the train driver or the detective but…just watch and see.'

And Francis tried to watch, but he was irritated with her.

'What's wrong, mum?'

'What do you mean?' His mother said crossly.

'You don't seem right.'

'I am fine. Worried about money, the usual,' she said, but Francis sensed that this was a different worry and felt that it was his job to press a little.

'Come on mum, you're grumpy. You always say I should tell you if there is something wrong. That has to work the other way too.'

'No it doesn't, I'm the adult.'

'So, you admit something is wrong.'

In the background Poirot was telling someone he wasn't French.

Rose sighed and quickly said, 'I have a lump.'

Francis was not sure what that meant. He had several lumps, he counted them in the bath after football matches and got up to thirteen once. Most of his lumps were on his shins, and he wondered if that's where his mum's lump was as well.

'Where is it?' he asked.

'Somewhere private,'

He realised he had no sense of his mother as private and he blushed.

'Won't it go away?'

'It isn't the sort of lump you get when you bang into something.'

'Have you been to the doctor?'

'Yes, I went last week when you were at school.'

'Why didn't you tell me?'

'I didn't want to worry you.'

Later in his life Francis would come to hate those words. He would instinctively believe them to be mildly, unconsciously manipulative, but currently Francis was twelve and comfortably innocent, and so he said, 'I'd rather know what's going on. So I can help. What did the Doctor say?'

'I have to have an X-ray and go to the hospital to see another Doctor. I am going to do that next week. Aunt Ruby is going to take me.'

Ruby and her husband, Ian, had a car and behaved as if this, and the fact that they didn't live in a council house, and used a sugar bowl, made them posh. They didn't often visit, which upset Grandad, but it didn't bother Francis. They did not like to bring their car to where Francis and Rose lived because they feared people might steal it, so if Aunt Ruby was coming that meant it was quite serious.

'Where is the lump, Mum?'

'On my breast, son,' she said as she leant in to hug him and he instinctively pulled away, worried in case he came into contact with the lump.

The next day at school Francis spent RE, Metalwork, and Geography wondering what would happen if he didn't have his mum. His grandad couldn't look after him, his grandad couldn't look after himself. Auntie Ruby and Uncle Ian didn't like him, they called him clever clogs and sneered when they said it, and they certainly wouldn't take both him and Grandad. They were the sort of people who talked about their carpet rather than walking on it until it was worn out, and they would never have had Grandad weeing on it. But they would probably still have taken Grandad over him, and he worried they might put him in a home. He had heard about homes and when people talked about them they made them sound like prisons for small people. When Francis thought about prisons he imagined indoors, not running, not going to the sea, not being on top of hills, and he couldn't think of anything worse. It was possible his father's family would take him in, but he had only met them twice and they didn't seem very nice. His mum had called them snobs and the only thing he remembered about them was that his aunties had ridiculous names like Lattice or Tangentia or something and none of them had ever married or smiled.

I'd run away, he thought to himself without any notion as to where away might be, but he was in the geography room when he thought it and the walls were covered in maps, so he knew that there was an awful lot of away to run to.

The day Rose went to the hospital Francis got into a fight at school. A boy, called Brian, had pulled his chair away from behind him as he went to sit down. Brian was just showing off, it was an easy laugh and Francis was an easy target because he was quiet and unpopular. Francis didn't actually hit the ground though, he staggered backwards and caught himself on another desk as he heard the other boys laugh. For the first time in his life he didn't think, he simply turned round and punched Brian in the ribs. The boys fell silent and one of the bigger ones stepped forward thinking this was his chance to practice his own punching, but Francis was too angry to be punched, the normal boundaries had been broken and the normal rules didn't apply. The bigger boy, Paul, who talked a lot about Karate, hesitated. Francis clenched his fists and began to move toward Paul, who stepped backwards and as he did so Francis swung a punch and caught him awkwardly on the side of his head. But the small moment of triumph was ruined when Francis shouted, 'just leave me alone.'

'You can't even take a joke,' said Paul as he rubbed at the side of his face and turned to the other boys to say, 'leave him, he's not worth it.'

On the upside, nobody pulled Francis' chair away again and Brian stayed away from him. On the downside, Francis had moved from odd outsider to guileless nutter.

       *   *   *

At the hospital Rose sat quietly on a plastic chair clutching her handbag and hoping against hope that good manners were a cure for cancer. The thin-faced, well-spoken doctor had said the words: 'We need to operate, Mrs. Broad, and after we have taken the lump away we need to give you a course of therapy to make sure it doesn't grow anywhere else.' As he spoke he looked over her shoulder and then out of the window. Rose could tell that he didn't actually want to be in the room with her and so she turned and looked out of the window, too.

'Will that be enough?' Rose asked.

'I think so,' the doctor sighed and drew his lips tightly together.

Rose recognised the same tone that she herself used when her father asked if she had enough money for the rent this month; a tone laced with more hope than judgement.

'I think we have caught it quite early, that means it hasn't had the chance to spread.'

His hands looked so clean and his skin was so pale that Rose wondered if he ever went outdoors. Perhaps there was too much work for a man like him to do to ever be able to go outdoors.

'And the treatment after the operation?' Rose asked because she knew that she would be asked by her father and her sister and eventually her son.

'It is like disinfecting a room after we have cleaned it.' The doctor said looking at her now, pleased perhaps to use a metaphor that he believed she would understand.

'Who will be doing the cleaning?' Rose asked.

'I will,' the doctor said, 'although other people will help with the chemotherapy afterwards.'

'Chemotherapy?' Rose asked. She knew that word. Bill, the best man at her wedding had had it. It turned him grey and he wilted and died. Now the fear came, swirling around in her polluted chest and she immediately felt embarrassed for asking. She was talking to a doctor, an educated man, a man who explained her cancer to her in terms of cleaning because that is what he thought she would understand. She would not cry, or faint or make a fuss. She would not be seen to make a fuss.

'I have a son. He is just a boy,' she said quietly.

'It will be all right Mrs Broad.' But his words didn't mean very much to her at all.

'When will you operate?'

'The sooner the better.'

'When?'

'Week after next, Mrs Broad.'

That night they had eggs, chips and spam for tea, and they ate in silence.

'Aunt Ruby will come and help when I am in hospital, keep an eye on you both.'

'We can manage,' said Francis. 'Can't we Grandad?'

Grandad didn't say anything, but later he cried at This Is Your Life even though he had no idea who the surprised person was.

'Aunt Ruby won't want to come here,' Francis whispered later as they watched the television.

'She will do what is needed,' Rose said firmly.

That night Francis had the worst of dreams. He dreamt he was on top of Nelson's Column, standing on Nelson's head. It was cold and dark and he was completely alone. He knew nobody would come and get him, or even know he was there, and that he would either die slowly from the cold and the hunger and the loneliness or he had to try to climb down alone and inevitably fall. He woke screaming as he lost his footing on Nelson's hat. His mother was there beside him, stroking his head, saying that he was safe, that she was there. He pretended to go back to sleep and waited for her to go. When he was alone he lay on his back and tried to think about what a life without his mother would be like, but he couldn't. All he could think about was how to get from the top of Nelson's Column without falling.

The next day Francis got home from school and asked his mum if she needed anything.

'No.'

'Would you like me to cook?'

'You can't cook,' she laughed.

'Neither can you but it doesn't stop you..'.

'Cheeky sod. I'm not an invalid. Go outdoors, tea at six.'

Francis went upstairs to put his running clothes on; and as he was digging around through his drawers he found some swimming trunks. He put them on under his track suit bottoms and packed his pants and a towel into his PE bag. He had no idea why he had decided today would be the day to begin swimming. Sometimes his body chose things and whatever part of him it was that turned things into words and thoughts just shrugged and accepted it. He did not say anything to his mother because she would have told him he couldn't swim in April and would then have mentioned drowning and more earnestly, catching a cold. He hoped the tide would be low, the water still and flat and he hoped the swimmer would be there to see him get in and to consider him brave. So, he slung his bag over his shoulder, ran down the stairs and straight out of the front door without even saying goodbye.

As he ran he revisited a recurrent question. What on earth was God doing giving his mother cancer? Was it a test? A punishment? Or maybe God wasn't quite as attentive as his mother imagined, maybe he had taken his eye off the ball and cancer had sneaked past, and now Rose was left trying to attract God's attention, politely of course, in the hope he might take it away again and drop it in the bin, or into a bad person. Not that Francis was entirely convinced by God, not deep down. Things seemed a bit too chaotic for anyone to be calling life a plan, although he was superstitious and cautious enough to know that now was not the time to stop believing. *Maybe it is me he is testing,* Francis thought, *maybe it is me who is failing, after all, I'm the one who is rubbish at holding on to parents.* He ran faster, on the off chance it might help and because he really wanted to get into the sea.

When he reached the promenade Francis could see that the tide was a long way out and he knew that even if he went to the water's edge he would still have to walk a long way to find water deep enough to swim in. He worried about leaving his clothes on the beach, which was littered with men digging in the sand for fish bait and he imagined how embarrassing it would be if someone stole his bag and he had to run home in his trunks to tell his mum he had lost his clothes and his trainers from Woolworths that Grandad had paid for and that he had not yet outgrown.

He walked slowly down toward the water, lost in these thoughts, until he found himself standing on the rippling wet sand, looking out to sea toward the point where the greys merged into the off white of the horizon. There was no part of him that wanted to get undressed now. He felt exposed in the middle of the beach, visible to everyone, sheltered from nothing.

'Long way to wade for a swim.' It was the swimmer, standing beside him, wearing actual clothes.

'Have you been in?'

'I had a short dip this morning. Not really feeling it this evening.'

'I was going to get in,' said Francis as he held up his bag as proof. 'When I was running down here I was hoping the sea would be flat and not too high because I was a bit nervous and I got here and it is flat and very, very low and…you think I'm making excuses don't you?'

'Do you see me in there?' the man said. 'Sometimes it's not for swimming.'

They stood quietly together staring at the water as Francis fidgeted with his bag.

'Something on your mind?' the swimmer asked.

And Francis thought, *well yeah, loads of stuff actually,* but he believed that usually when a grown up asked you a question, it was some sort of trick, and they either thought they knew the answer already or they were going to criticise you for whatever answer you gave, so the correct answer to the question posed by the stranger would be a shrug or a 'no' or 'If you swam straight ahead would you reach France?' or 'Have you ever seen a dolphin or a seal or a shark?' or 'How cold is the water now?'

But there was something about the water, maybe even the gentle, rhythmic breathing noise it made as it edged toward them, that made him say very quietly; 'My mum has cancer.'

7

Francis had begun writing letters to an imaginary friend, a girl called Patricia when he was nine. She lived in America and he had decided that she spent a lot of time outdoors, just like himself, where she would go walking over hills to a little lake where she would go swimming. He still wrote to her most Sundays. He felt that Patricia would be kind and certainly cleverer than him, and so when he wrote he always felt he needed to be the best version of himself in order to encourage her, even though she didn't exist, to write back.

I ran to the beach today, school was bad but that seems to make me run faster. I like it when I can smell the sea. I expect you run quicker than I do. Do you run toward your lake? Can you smell the water like I can or is it different? I have never seen a lake. My mother is ill. She has cancer. Cancer seems to like our house. I expect she will be ok. It is my job to help her. When she used to say I was the man of the house I always felt she was joking. Now it seems true.

He liked being able to tell her things that could not be said elsewhere. And as he wrote he liked to imagine what she would say in her reply. *We don't choose who we are,* he imagined she would write, *even though we like to think we do.*

As the day of Rose's surgery grew closer, Francis began to resist the urge to go back outdoors after tea and instead he would scribble off another letter to Patricia and then go down to the front room to sit with his mum. They would watch American detective shows and British sit coms; *Kojak and On The Buses. Columbo and Are You Being Served.* They didn't laugh at the comedy or speak about the detectives. They sat in silence, staring at the small screen and waiting for bedtime.

Sometimes as they were watching television, Francis would look at his mum and try to see signs of the cancer. When his father had it, he would hear people say things like, 'it spreads so quickly,' and he would be reminded of the water he once spilled on the kitchen table that raced in all directions until everything was wet, or they would say 'it's very aggressive' and he'd imagine a cancer shouting from inside his father's skin like the angry wrestlers did on Saturday afternoon TV. His father had changed colour and become thinner, he breathed more heavily and looked tired all the time. But Rose was not changing colour. Perhaps her cancer wasn't as angry, he thought, but he tried to stay close to her anyway; always watching, always there ready to help.

One evening, out of the blue, Rose said, 'this room needs decorating. The paper is all yellow at the top, from your father's smoking. Maybe when I get out of the hospital…'

They were both silent, until Francis said, 'I would like to be a better swimmer.'

'You're better than me,' said Rose, who had never seen a reason to get into water that wasn't in a bath.

'Sometimes when I go to the beach, I watch this man who swims a lot. He is very good; he never seems to have to stop

63

to get his breath back or see where he is. He looks very sort of smooth, in the water. When I swim, I am going to copy him.'

'I never knew you went swimming?'

'I don't…but when I do…I mean…'

'Does this man talk to you?'

'He's in the sea mum, swimming.'

'But when he gets out.'

He swims for a long time. I'd like to be able to do that.' He said, not lying.

'That's good, dear,' she said, staring at the wall. 'I think the kitchen might need decorating, too.'

'Maybe,' said Francis. 'No rush though, best get the operation over with first.'

'Tuesday son, I'm going in on Tuesday.'

'That's quite soon,' said Francis and his eyes begin to prickle and burn.

The next day, after school, Francis ran to the beach. When he got there it was mid-tide, the sun was low over the water and the wind was gentle. The waves were small and appeared preoccupied with heading across the bay rather than in toward the shore. The beach was empty and Francis could see the swimmer's bag and clothes stacked neatly beside the slipway. He had decided that today he would undress and put his clothes, if not next to the swimmer's, at least quite near them; and then when he had the chance he would ask him for some swimming advice. So, Francis hurriedly undressed and ran down into the water, which was so cold that he couldn't put his face under for fear it would freeze. He lasted about five minutes in there. Every time he dipped his shoulders under and started to do the breaststroke it felt like his chest was about to explode so he pulled himself along the sandy bottom, just as he had done as a child, and then hurried along back to his clothes. He shivered as he rubbed his towel across his goosebumps, and as he did so he scanned the horizon to see if he could see the swimmer. He dragged on his clothes, his sweaty top sticking to his skin, making him feel even colder, and as he was sat doing up his trainers he saw the man emerge from the water and head up the beach toward him.

'You look cold young man.'

'I'm ok.'

'It's ok to be cold, you know that right?'

'Yeah, it felt colder today, not sure why.' *Colder than what,* thought Francis, *I've not been in the water since I was four.* He looked away from the swimmer half expecting to be mocked.

'What sort of day have you had?' The swimmer was towelling himself down now. Still not rushing anything he did.

'Ok.'

The swimmer looked at him, 'Ok? What does that mean? Has it been a day where good things happened? Where bad things happened? What stands out? What is the best part of the day so far?'

'Running down here, I suppose.'

'You not enjoying school?'

'Not really.'

'Too hard?'

'You could say that?'

'You got friends?'

Francis considered lying and telling him that he had a really good friend called Patricia and that she lived in America, but he didn't and just said, 'Not many, I don't really fit in. Never have.'

'Probably no consolation, but that gets easier the older you get, honest,' said the swimmer as he pulled on a heavy woollen jumper and matching hat.

'Yeah,' said Francis, thinking that the next time, he needs to bring another top and maybe ask for a woolly hat for his birthday.

'It really does. You'll find a tribe.' Which made Francis think of westerns and Apache and riding bareback horses to catch up with a wagon train.

'How's your mum?'

'No change,' Francis said quickly, realising he felt irritated but didn't know why. 'Can I ask a swimming question?'

'Sure,' said the swimmer, who was now taking his trunks off behind a giant towel.

'If you could give me one tip to be better at swimming, what would it be?'

'You could try swimming,' said the swimmer.

'I do swim,' said Francis, and immediately realised how childish that made him sound.

'You get in the water, which is a good start, and you immerse yourself, which is useful for swimming, but you don't actually propel yourself for very long or put your face in the water or move your arms about…'

'I do,' said Francis indignantly, 'sometimes.'

'You need goggles. Then you need to practice the front crawl without turning your head from side to side as though the sea is a giant wasp and you are trying not to have your face stung. Then you need to learn to breathe out under the water.'

'What sort of goggles?' was all Francis could think to say.

'Ones that don't leak are good.'

Francis felt stupid for asking that and was cross with himself. 'You look cold, want a hot drink?' The swimmer said, offering Francis his thermos flask.

'I'm ok thanks. You look like you need it more,' said Francis with a touch of anger.

'I probably do mate. I'm really cold today.'

'I thought you didn't get cold.'

'Why would you think that?'

'Because you swim all winter and you act like…like you don't get cold…'

'Well, I'm freezing now and you'll never hear me say it isn't anything other than cold out there.'

'So why do you do it?'

'Why do you?'

'Well, like you just said, I don't…and I don't know why I want to.'

Francis looked at the water, it was many things but mainly it was big, endless even, and if he imagined for a moment closing his eyes and opening them to find himself out on the horizon, he would feel the fear in his chest almost cripple him. He liked the colours, he liked how he felt as he lay on his back and let the waves push him up and down and he thought that perhaps he wanted to be a bit like the man he was talking to. But he couldn't say that, how stupid that would be, so he stood up and walked away. When he got to the top of the jetty he turned and saw that the swimmer was looking up toward him.

'Maybe see you tomorrow?' Francis shouted, but the swimmer didn't hear him.

8

Rose was in hospital for ten days. Francis went to school every day but he was like a shadow passing through the walls and the playground. Aunt Ruby was helping and was, by her standards, trying to make an effort, although she was unable to stop herself from humiliating Grandad and was always asking him why he could not set off for the toilet sooner and with some exasperation saying loudly, 'Rose should have told me you were this bad. There are pads you can wear, you know.' Grandad did not fully understand what she meant by pads, but he felt the shame sharply enough to cry during *Crossroads*. She would spend most of her time sitting in the kitchen reading the *Daily Express* and told her husband loudly when he came to pick her up: 'I sit in here because it doesn't smell quite so much'.

When Rose came home, Grandad cried and Francis made her a very weak cup of tea, which she drank anyway. She looked thinner, even though she hadn't been gone long, and it made her look quite well, or would have done if her skin didn't look so yellow and if she didn't keep falling asleep in front of

Coronation Street.

'I need to get my strength up for the chemotherapy,' Rose would say to them, 'but I'm not doing press ups and I am not coming out running with you.'

Seeing his mum dozing on the sofa frightened Francis. He could feel the fear rising from the pit of his stomach to the edges of his skin and no amount of running seemed to help, but the constant buzz that coursed through his bones did drive him into the sea with more determination. He was now getting straight into the water and putting his face under, even though he still didn't have any goggles. He'd seen the swimmer three times while his mum had been in hospital, but they didn't talk much. The swimmer was staying in for longer now that it was getting lighter and warmer, and Aunty Ruby was strict about him being home in time for tea. When they did have some time together they talked about the currents, the colours of the water and how it would appear differently depending on the tide.

On the third day after Rose had come home from hospital the buzz became too much for Francis and so he headed out earlier than normal and arrived at the beach the same time as the swimmer.

'Why do you swim so much?' Francis asked, as they sat down together.

'I think there will be some clouds along soon, might be tough conditions out there.'

The sky was clear, the sea was still and Francis wondered if he had asked a silly question.

'What do you do?' Francis though he would try a different approach.

'I work in a library,' the swimmer said.

'That sounds great, I love libraries, although my aunty says that libraries are for boring people.'

'Does she now. Well I think libraries are for interesting people, the more time people spend near books they more likely they are to start to absorb the knowledge they contain through osmosis,' he smiled at his own joke even though Francis didn't understand it.

A dark grey cloud had started to roll in slowly from the horizon and Francis wondered what osmosis meant, but he didn't want to ask

'Libraries are a bit like the beach, continued the swimmer. 'They get very busy every now and then, but the rest of the time they are the domain of the committed. I like it when it is busy but I prefer it when it is quiet. More time to think. Having that space, either between the shelves or in the sea, helps me to work things though in my mind, helps me to process what is going on inside my head…some days I need to swim hard and other days I just want to float along. Maybe it's like that with you and running?'

'Maybe' said Francis, not really sure what the man was on about but knowing that what he said seemed to make sense.

'What's your name?' the swimmer asked.

'I'm Francis.'

'Do people call you Frank?'

'No.'

'I might.' Said the swimmer as he laughed, 'Anyhow, how's your mum getting on?'

'She is home. She had the operation and now she is going to have chemotherapy. That will kill the cancer they say.'

'I hope so,' said the swimmer.

At home when they talked about the cancer, they didn't

talk about hoping it would be ok, they only ever said that it would be ok. Perhaps they did this to stop him from asking what he knew he wanted to ask; 'but what if it isn't, what if the chemotherapy doesn't kill the cancer? Would there be another plan? Another operation?'

'I don't have a dad.' Francis blurted out.

'Yeah, I sort of guessed that.'

'How?'

'You never mentioned one.'

'He died.'

'I'm sorry.'

'He'd already left us before that though, so…'

'So?'

'So, it wasn't as sad as it should have been if he hadn't already of left us.'

Francis looked away and stared at the grey-green water. His eyes began to fill and his lungs hurt.

'It's hard, isn't it?' the swimmer said gently.

Francis just carried on staring at the water.

'Not knowing is hard, being afraid is hard and I think not having any power to do anything to help, that is really, really hard isn't it?' The swimmer was hunched forward, looking at Francis.

'It isn't fair. I want to help but…' Francis said and waited to be told that life wasn't fair and maybe some rubbish about ill winds and silver clouds or too many cooks spoiling the stupid broth, but there was nothing.

'I'm not stupid,' Francis continued, 'I know bad things happen, and mum always says there are people worse off than us and I'm not in a competition, but this isn't fair because there is nothing I can do, there is never ever anything I can do. When my dad kept leaving and then coming back, there was nothing I could do. I wanted to change the locks, but I couldn't even reach them. When he left for the last time, I couldn't make sure he stayed away. When Grandad started getting old and confused there was nothing I could do except keep telling him it was Wednesday. And now, mum is ill, there is nothing I can do. I just…bob about in it all.'

'What does your mum say?'

'She says to pray but…'

'But what?'

'But that doesn't even make sense.' Francis paused, the cloud now covered the whole sky, and the sea was getting darker and noisier.

'Why doesn't it make sense?'

'Because if there is a God, and he gave mum the cancer and me the rubbish dad, why would he take it away if I ask? He either has a reason to do things or he doesn't. Why would he change his mind? Because a twelve--year-old boy, whose own dad didn't even like him enough to carry on living with, is asking?' Francis stood up and picked up his duffel bag without looking at the swimmer.

'You're right, it isn't fair.' said the swimmer. 'And for what it's worth, if I were you, I would want to find something I could do to change things too.'

*   *   *

The chemotherapy began a fortnight later. The most notable effect to Francis was that his mum seemed more tired when he got home from school, and so he did less running because he wanted to be near her when she dozed off with her head on the kitchen table. Her yellow skin had begun to turn grey and she had started wearing a headscarf because her fine, greying hair was falling out. She also seemed to have lost even more weight, only now it didn't make her look healthy. To Francis these things announced that the cancer had moved in and was now completely redecorating their lives.

The end of the school year came and went, and with it a school report that remarked on Francis being a bit of a dreamer and not concentrating on his work as much as he should. To his surprise his mother didn't seem to mind very much and that worried him, so he apologised, promising to do better next year, whilst silently promising the universe that he would be the cleverest person in the school if she just got better.

It wasn't until the end of the first week of the summer holidays that Francis saw the swimmer again. Rose was into her fourth week of chemotherapy and Francis had borrowed money from his grandad to buy her a headscarf from British Home Stores. She kept telling him he needed to go out and play, that he was spending too much time indoors, but he felt a duty to his mum, and so he stayed at home and wrote to Patricia. He always wanted to tell her about the sea or the summer but then he would write about his mum. He would tell her how she was getting thin and how was tired all of the time. How he had heard her being sick in the toilet and it had scared him. Then he would ask her what she had been doing – swimming he imagined – and ask how her parents were, and whether she believed in God?

He thought she would say, yes, because it is too hard not to.

One morning, whilst he was making his mum a cup of weak tea, Rose said to him, 'will you please go out and play, you are getting under my feet,' even though she was sitting down at the kitchen table when she said it. He was out of the house before 8 a.m. and he had decided that because he hadn't been running for a while he would take the longer route to the beach. He ran out past the village into the expanse of marshland that lay beyond the farms, at that time of the day there was no one else around and the only sounds he could hear were the calls of the gulls and the sigh of the sea carried on the breeze. He stopped to catch his breath and felt first alone and then lonely. If he had been nearer home he would have immediately turned around and gone back to hug his mum, holding her as tight as he could so she couldn't fall over, telling her that he would always be there to look after her. But he wasn't, so he walked a little while until his eyes stopped burning and his faced had dried.

From the marshes he joined the sea wall and he began to jog along it again, looking outward to the sea, and that was when he spotted the swimmer, a long way out, swimming slowly from the cliffs in the east, looking like he was aiming for the jetty where Francis had seen him that very first time as he tried to escape the crashing waves. Francis ran on as fast as he could and by the time he was breathlessly getting changed into his swimming trunks he could see that the swimmer was parallel to the jetty but still a long way out. It was low tide, and although the summer sun had warmed the sand on the beach the water was still cold and as he waded out from the shallows to the deeper water beyond he felt it's cold sting creep up over his skin. By the time the swimmer had arrived next to him he had at least got under the water and managed to do a few strokes, his efforts helping to dispel some of the chill from his body.

'I have something for you,' said the swimmer as he treaded water beside Francis, 'keep practicing, I'll be back in a minute.'

Francis lay back in the water and stared up at the small summer clouds, testing himself to see how long he could stay afloat before having to move his arms and legs to stop himself from going under.

'Here, try these,' said the swimmer as he tossed a blue pair of goggles at the floating Francis.

They hit Francis on his chest and he immediately sunk beneath the surface. He rose, thrashing his arms about and spluttering. Once he had regained his composure, he scooped the goggles up from the water and pulled them over his head, all the while frantically kicking his legs to keep himself steady. The swimmer came up next to him and pulled on the rubber straps until Francis could feel the goggles biting into the skin around his eyes.

'Go on then, off you go, let's see how you get on now.'

Francis took a deep breath, put his face in the water and began to swim. Within five minutes he was swimming twenty, then twenty-five, then thirty strokes without stopping. He kept going and going, turning his face and blowing out the salty water he had swallowed, until he was out of breath and realised that he was on his own. He quickly scanned the sea around him but there was no sign of the swimmer, he was out of his depth and was starting to panic when he saw the swimmer standing on the beach, watching him. He calmed, he knew he was safe, he knew that if he couldn't make it back that the swimmer would help him, and so he put his face back under and slowly pulled himself back to the shallows where he stood and waded back up toward the beach.

'Thank you so much,' said Francis, as he took off the

goggles and handed them to the swimmer, 'they make a real difference don't they.'

'They are all yours, keep hold of them. Now get yourself dry and we will have a cup of tea.'

Francis rubbed himself down, planted himself next to the swimmer and eagerly wrapped his cold hands around the steaming mug of tea he had been offered.

'How's your mum doing?' the swimmer asked.

'Not great.'

'And how are you?'

'Ok, I guess. I just wish it was me having the treatment, that I could do it for her.'

'I don't think your mum would want you to go through that, would she?'

Francis blew across the steam rising from his mug and then surprised himself by saying, 'I feel as though I am letting her down. Like it is my job to look after her and I'm not.'

The swimmer didn't respond, but Francis could hear his words in his head anyway, words like 'you can't' and 'it isn't your fault,' and he sighed at the imaginary conversation and pinched the inside of his leg in irritation.

'Can I ask you a question? You might think it a silly question though?' the swimmer said, breaking their silence.

'Is it about why I stop swimming after twenty yards?'

'That wouldn't be a silly question' smiled the swimmer.

'Go on then.'

'How long do you think you will live?'

'I dunno.' Francis pulled a face; it was not something he had ever thought about.

'Think for a minute, I know it is unpredictable, you could get run over by a bus or hit by an asteroid...'

'Or get cancer, everyone else seems to.'

'Or that, yes, but you might not, and you live in a country where life expectancy is pretty good so…how long?'

'Sixty-five maybe?'

'Why do you say that?'

'Grandad retired at sixty-five, he is seventy-two now and really, really old. I don't want to wet myself and forget what day it is.'

'But in fifty years' time they may have found a cure for the forgetfulness or know how to stop it happening, and maybe having seen your grandad struggle you might make different choices.'

'What, like sit nearer the toilet?'

'Something like that,' the swimmer laughed, 'I mean do you think there were things your grandad might have done differently when he retired?'

Francis shrugged. He didn't want to criticise his grandad. It felt unkind and disloyal, but he did just sit down for a very long time and maybe that didn't help.

'Life expectancy now for men is seventy-four. By the time you are fifty it will probably be over eighty.'

'I don't want to live until I'm eighty,' said Francis for whom thirty seemed over the hill. 'I'll be decrepit. Bits of me will be falling off.'

'So, you'd settle for sixty-five?'

'Yeah, I think so…I mean on *Tomorrow's World* they say that there will be pills that keep you young…'

'And jet packs?'

'Yeah, I would like a jet pack.'

'Instead of running everywhere?'

Francis shook his head. 'I'd still run.'

'So,' the swimmer said, leaning toward Francis who was staring into his tea, 'here is the silly question...'

'I thought you'd already asked it.'

'No that was just a preliminary one.'

'Go on then.'

'If I told you that you were going to live until you were eighty-five and then die relatively painlessly in your sleep, but your mother will be cured of her cancer if you sign away twenty years of your life, and as a consequence die at sixty-five, would you do it?'

'Of course,' said Francis immediately. 'I would sign away fifty years, a hundred...'

'You don't have a hundred, and never offer more than you are asked for.' The swimmer looked serious and was staring intently at Francis intently.

Would I give away years of my life? Francis thought. *Of course I would. For one thing they were old years, I probably wouldn't enjoy them, and I might be wetting himself by then, and anyway they were a long way away. Old people mostly wore cardigans and looked exhausted. Giving away old years is easy.*

'Would the cancer stay away?'

'Good question, young man. Let's suppose that it would stay away for at least twenty years. It may stay away longer but we don't know. But this cancer, this one, would go and not come back.'

'She'd be in her seventies and I'd be in my thirties,' said Francis as he felt the steam from his tea condensing on his face. 'I would happily give away twenty years of my life for my mum, but I suppose it's easy to sacrifice something that isn't real isn't it?'

'What if it were real, Francis? What if I told you that the

cancer would go away if you agreed to give up twenty years of your life?' The swimmer was staring intently at Francis, his grey eyes mirroring the colour of the sea.

'I'd say you were mad.'

'Of course, but after that, would you take the deal?'

'Yes, I would. Definitely. But how would I know it wasn't a trick?'

'You'd know if your mum got better, wouldn't you?'

'But what if she didn't?'

'Then this was just a silly game, and you live for as long as you live.'

The swimmer turned and pulled out an envelope from his bag. He tore it open and offered the piece of paper it contained to Francis. Putting down his mug of tea, Francis took the paper and read the words typed on it: *I Francis Broad agree to donate twenty years of my life in exchange for my mum (Rose Broad) recovering from breast cancer.* There was a dotted line at the bottom with the words signature and date printed on it, and for the first time in his life Francis realised that fear and excitement were the same thing.

'Is this…what is this?'

'Well, it is whatever you think I suppose. It could be a small psychological experiment, it could be a stupid and cruel game, particularly if your mum stays ill or gets worse, or it could be…magic? Thing is, you have to decide what to do now, because that piece of paper is real even if you don't think anything else is.'

'I could tear it up,' Francis said and instantly felt like a fool.

'You could, but that won't mean you hadn't seen it, would it?'

'And if I sign this, my mum will get better.'

The swimmer looked at him and waited.

'Is this some sort of test?' asked Francis.

'I suspect most things feel like a test at the moment son, don't they?'

That was true, everything felt like a test to Francis; even when he passed them it just meant there would be another test, and when he thought about who it was who was testing him, it seemed to him to be some version of a god or the universe or some all-seeing, never-satisfied, teasing type of school teacher. He didn't believe in magic, at least he didn't think he did, but he did believe that he was under surveillance in some way, perhaps by the sky or sea or the non-existent Patricia, he did feel he was constantly having to prove himself. To earn his place on this planet that he had only just about managed to scrape his way onto in the first place.

'I'll sign it,' Francis said flatly, and he looked up to see the swimmer holding out a pen. Francis took it from him and signed his name. 'What's the date?'

'August 2nd.'

Francis wrote the date, handed the pen back to the swimmer and sat staring at the piece of hope he held in his hand.

'I'm not going to be around this summer,' the swimmer said, as he took the piece of paper from Francis and placed it back in the envelop 'I'm going to be away for a while.'

Francis would be sad about that later, when he was at home in bed, thinking about what had happened, wondering how on earth the swimmer knew his second name, but now he simply said, 'That's nice.'

'By the time I get back I expect to see you swimming the length of this bay, ok?', said the swimmer as he stood up and shouldered his bag. 'Take care of yourself Francis; your mum will be fine, try to make sure you are too, eh?'

Francis nodded and watched as the swimmer strolled off down the promenade. He didn't know what had just happened. He had either just saved his mum or he had just found himself at the heart of a coincidence that made him feel both more powerful than he had ever imagined possible or more responsible than he could bear, because as it turned out, his mother got better.

They celebrated at Christmas. They drank cheap fizzy wine and orange juice mixed together. She cried after two drinks and Grandad weed in the living room, not because his incontinence was getting worse but because he had drunk too much. Rose looked better through winter, she had put on a little more weight and her skin had stopped being grey and then stopped being yellow. Her recovery further cemented Rose's sense of herself as one of life's winners. She had everything she had dreamed of: a son, a roof, the absence of cancer. What more could a woman ask for?

And Francis was laced with relief. He would not go into care, not be completely alone and he had, it seemed, looked after his mother. He stopped writing to Patricia because she wasn't real and he gradually stopped going to the beach, perhaps because it was real, and he watched his mother; kept guard, ever vigilant, primed to act, just in case something bad happened.

9

Francis was forty-three years of age and as he swam, and was alone with his thoughts, he reasoned he was now two thirds of the way through his life. Swimming was one of the things that offered him the illusion of slowing down time, so he did it most days, but time passed quickly, nonetheless.

It was a cold and cloudless Thursday in March. He always finished work early on Thursdays and he wondered if Rose remembered and if that was why she was calling him now. He was at home, putting a clean towel in his bag for a swim, hurriedly filling a flask with coffee when his phone rang. He was a little irritated and later he would remember that and feel ashamed.

'Francis, the cancer is back. The doctor says it is in me. Really in me.'

'In you,' there was no inflection, he knew what she meant, he had just said the words to fill the unbearable space.

'I'm sorry son.'

'Why are you saying sorry to me?'

'Because I know this will hurt you, I know you are already

hurting son, but I think I had extra time, and I am grateful.'

Grateful, always grateful. She was right though, he was already hurting and she had had extra time.

'Come and stay mum?'

'Alright son, but let's not make a fuss.'

The next day he drove to Birchington to pick her up. To his eyes she was greyer and a little bit slower in everything she did, but he did as he was told and didn't make a fuss.

'We are both lucky with what we have Francis,' she said on the drive back, 'don't ever think otherwise.' Then without barely drawing a breath, 'There isn't anything they can do really. They said I could have chemotherapy and it might give me a few more weeks but when I had it before and it made me sick. I remember trying to cook your tea and running to the kitchen sink to throw up. I don't want that again son.'

They drove in silence for a little while before she said. 'Do you know what I liked about your dad?'

'Nothing as far as I can recall?' He smiled.

'He had a car. I thought that was...I don't know what I thought it was...glamourous I think.'

'It was a little Ford Anglia, wasn't it?'

'I don't know. It was green and it smelt of cigarettes.' She looked sad and Francis didn't speak for a few miles.

'Rae is really looking forward to seeing you mum. And so is Vic.'

'They don't mind me coming?'

'Of course not.'

Rose smiled and looked out of the window.

At Francis's house Rose mostly sat in a chair pushed back against the wall in the living room, reading crime novels and doing word puzzles. In between times she dozed off and let life go on around her. Sometimes Francis saw her wince when she moved, mostly she faded into the walls like a sea fret over the morning sea but she came to life when Rae returned home from school. Rae was nine; old enough to know what illness looked like and what it was going to do, but still young enough to give her Nanny a hug as soon as she got in and to tell her something about her day.

'I saw a dead pigeon and we played rounders, I didn't hit the ball. Do you know what H2O is?'

Rae would keep on talking and Rose would listen with enthusiasm. To Francis' eyes though, Rose seemed to shrink a tiny bit more each day. He would catch himself looking at her as she slept in the chair and he imagined the air around her being different somehow; toxic, stale. He wanted to open a window to let it out, to let her breath, and deep down he believed the cancer was his fault, because of what he had done. She was ill because of him.

'I'd like to go home son.' Rose said after three weeks,

'Why?'

'I want to be in my own place.'

He was hurt and relieved. When he told Rae that her Nanny was going to go home she said, 'that makes sense daddy, we can visit her can't we? Bring her things.'

'Why do you think it makes sense?'

'People like their own homes best...and...'

'And what sweetheart?'

'She is different to when she came.'

So, Francis took Rose home. He bought her food and stocked up the cupboards and fridge, promising to come back the following week. That was how it continued for four months. At first all three of them came to visit. Then it was just Rae and Francis. Rae would bring the light with her, bounding in, hugging her Nanny, telling her about a mean girl at school or about the book about cats she had been reading or about how she was going to start piano lessons soon.

'Your daddy wanted piano lessons,' Rose said.

'Did I?'

'You probably did Daddy,' Rae said siding with her Nanny, 'that's why you are buying them for me. Parents always want things for their children they wanted for themselves.'

Rose laughed. 'You are clever Rae,' she said, 'cleverer than your dad.'

'Oi you two, I'm still here you know.'

But after a couple of months Francis noted that Rae was less keen to visit and when she arrived she would hesitate slightly before hugging her Nanny, bending slowly, not burying her head into Rose's shoulder as she used to, facing away from the yellowing skin.

Before they left Rae went to the toilet and Rose said, 'you should stop bringing her here now son, she doesn't need to see this.'

'See what?'

'This,' she stared at Francis, 'I want her to remember... something better. Please.'

On the drive home Francis said to Rae, 'she will get worse you know.'

Rae didn't say anything.

'I wonder if perhaps you shouldn't come next time.'

'I don't want to let her down.'

'I think your Nanny wants you to remember her as strong. I wonder if...and I know this sounds a bit funny...but I wonder if not visiting her would actually be kind?'

'You're just saying that.'

'Why would I?'

'Because you think I'm a child.'

'You are a child, but I don't think that is a bad thing.'

'You think I am a child, and I shouldn't see someone who is dying.' Rae started crying.

'No, I'm asking, I'm asking your opinion, what do you think Nanny wants? What do you think she needs? I think you are the most important person in the world to her and I think she cares very much about what you think of her, what you see when you look at her. What you will remember. That is what I think, and I wonder what you think?'

Rae visited one more time, two weeks later. Rose was smaller still, stooped over in her chair. She was on stronger pain killers and kept falling asleep, but when she was awake she kept saying sorry to Rae,

'I'm sorry sweetheart, I keep dozing off and you have come all this way. I didn't sleep very well last night.' And then, 'I'm sorry Rae, this is your Saturday, you should be playing with your friends.' And finally, desperately, 'When I'm better sweetheart I'll make it up to you, we will play whatever game you want, for as long as you want and I won't fall asleep until bedtime.' And a few minutes later she fell asleep again.

'You've done well Rae,' Francis whispered, 'I'm proud of you, but it's enough now.'

Rae nodded.

*   *   *

Before Francis had turned forty-four Rose had retreated completely into her drying skin and had shrunk inexorably from her compact world. Francis was visiting on his own now.

'What do you do mum?' he asked, 'what do you do when I am not here?'

'I watch the TV. I read. I do the crosswords. The woman next door brings me dinner and I don't eat it. And I remember.'

'Remember what?'

'You running around. Used to drive your grandad mad. You never stopped, just like now. We were happy.'

Were we? wondered Francis.

'Weren't we son?' said Rose, as if she were reading his mind.

'Yes Mum, I don't know how you did it, but yes we were.'

Sometimes they watched TV in the afternoon together. Once they watched an old episode of *Columbo* that they had watched together when he was young.

'Remember this one?' he asked.

'Not really,' she said.

After a few long hours, she would say, 'You should get back to your girls' son, it's boring for you here.'

'No, it isn't.'

'Go on, leave me in peace, you stop me doing what I do.'

'I'll stay for a little while,' he said. But she was already asleep. He waited for her to wake before he left and then he drove home in the twilight; numb, dutiful, guilty.

The following weekend she had shrunk into the cardigan he had bought her for Christmas, it looked four sizes too big now. Her skin seemed thinner too, she was close to transparent. He kissed her head and it was cold.

'How is my granddaughter?'

'She is good, sends her love.'

'She's so bright,' Rose said. 'Bright as a star. Brighter than you were at that age.'

'I know mum,'

'But you are bright too son, and now look at you, you have a family of your own.' She was out of breath, every sentence exhausting her.

'Have you eaten?' Francis asked.

'There is some chicken in the fridge, next door brought it round.'

'Have you eaten, is what I asked?'

'No. I'm not hungry.'

'What did the doctor say?'

'Said I can go into hospital if I like, but who the bloody hell wants to go into hospital? He told me to try not to get a chest infection and I said to him that I'll try not to break both my legs as well.'

'You should be listening to what they say though, Mum.'

'I would if they weren't so ridiculous…do you remember… you wanted to be a doctor once.'

'I think you wanted me to be one Mum, that's not quite the same.'

Rose's shoulders gave a little shrug that hinted at a smile.

They sat like that for what felt like hours and Francis wondered how many times he would be in this house again.

'I'm scared son.' Rose said.

'What of, Mum?'

'Of dying. What if there isn't a heaven?'

He stroked her bony arm. 'You always told me there was a heaven, why would you change your mind now? What do you think heaven is like, Mum?'

'I think it's good,' she said, 'and I think you probably see everyone there you want to see.'

'Everyone?'

'Everyone who went before you.' She paused, breathing heavily now. 'But there is one thing that worries me.'

'What's that, Mum?'

'How do they get everyone in?'

'What do you mean?'

'There are an awful lot of dead people son. How does God get them all in?'

'He's God, Mum, isn't he? He can do anything.'

'That's right son, he gave me you, didn't he? And then when you were born, he made you better didn't he?'

Rose closed her eyes, exhausted now by the conversation. She dozed in her chair for over an hour, her head down, her mouth slack. Sometimes she would jerk herself awake for a moment, make a sound, like a question mark, and then her head would flop back down again. Francis watched her chest move feebly up and down wondering if she might just stop breathing while he sat there, afraid of that moment but sure it was coming.

She roused herself. 'Do you still swim?' she said out of the blue.

'I do.'

'I wasn't scared when you used to go to the sea. Perhaps I should have been. I used to worry more about you crossing the roads. I still do. Why don't you go for a swim now, son. Give me a chance to get some peace.'

'It's been a long time since I swam in that bit of sea mum.'

'Go on then, and afterwards, you can come back to say bye and get home to those girls of yours.'

'You are one of my girls, Mum,' he said but he didn't think she heard him, so he lent over, put his arms round her thin shoulders and whispered, 'I love you mum.'

10

'It's not too late to change your mind,' Rose had said as soon as he was up.

Francis hugged her, trying to look as though this was as hard for him as it was for her and when he stepped out of the door into the fresh autumnal air, he had never felt so excited in all his life.

Francis was eighteen and his grandad had died six months earlier, in the middle of a surprise March snowfall. The death certificate said pneumonia, but to Francis it looked as though he had slowly shrunk from the world, faculty by faculty, until only a miniature ball of flesh was left; a ball of flesh which had then forgotten how to breathe. It was a small funeral, held at the old village church. Francis liked how peoples footsteps echoed through the space and the way the light came through the stained-glass windows and dappled the small gathering with shapes of colour. The vicar seemed serious and sad when he talked about Grandad, but Francis didn't cry. He felt his grandad had been released from something gnawing and unpleasant and he believed the old man had lasted longer than he himself was going to. If Francis had needed any more motivation to go and live, it came from the death of his exhausted and incontinent grandad.

Leaving the house he had grown up in felt symbolic of something new and fresh, even though the handle had fallen off his heavy suitcase halfway to the station and he'd had to carry it in his arms like a large, sleeping child. Rose had cried on the platform and for the whole journey Francis kept thinking of her still standing there, waiting for him to change his mind and return. At his halls of residence, a tall tower block in the centre of London, he shuffled through the bustling corridors to his small room which contained a single bed, a pine wardrobe, a desk and a sink. He threw his suitcase down on the bed, opened it and began to unpack. At the bottom of the case he found his mum's old cardigan with a note that read: 'I'm proud of you, this is here, just in case, and so am I. xx.'

Francis wondered what his mum would be doing now. *Washing,* he decided, *she would be washing clothes at the kitchen sink. Crying.* He slid the case, with the cardigan still in it, under the bed and glanced out of the window. He could see buildings and people and life and for a moment it occurred to him that he might be in the wrong place, the wrong world, and as he was thinking this a boy tapped lightly on the door of the room to attract Francis' attention.

'Hello, I'm Ben. Do you fancy a cup of coffee?'

That evening Francis, Ben and a girl called Joy, a tall Mancunian with a tattoo of red flowers on her arm and a permanently available sneer to call upon should something or someone require it, sat in Ben's room listening to music and drinking horrible tasting wine.

'I got kicked out of my family home because I am gay,' Ben said. 'My sister outed me at the dinner table on Christmas Day.'

'Why did she do that?' asked Joy.

'Because I wouldn't give her money not to.'

'Classy.'

'I know right, and then straight after that my dad kicked me out.'

'Because you're gay?'

'He has strong feelings about, and I'm quoting here, sodomy.'

'What about your mum? Francis asked.

'I don't know her position on sodomy.' Ben chuckled. 'She sends me letters sometimes though, with a fiver in them. I should send them back really but I...I guess she feels bad, she struggles with dad as well...after they kicked me out, I went and stayed with my grandad. He is great. We spent the summer making things together. We made three chairs and a cabinet. He is a kind man. I'm lucky to have him.'

'My dad is a bully,' said Joy, 'he expected me to be a lawyer like him and I came here to spite him.'

'I never really had a dad,' Francis said quietly. 'Sounds like I got off lightly.'

'Sister?' asked Joy.

'Nope, just me and my mum and until recently, my grandad. I'd like to make my mum proud.' He blushed. 'She gave up a lot for me, you know?'

'So what are you doing here?'

Francis hesitated, self-conscious, he was not used to speaking about his life.

'My mum never had much of a life, she just looked after

me and my grandad and worried about money…I know this is stupid but I thought that kind of sacrifice deserved that I at least try and…live? Staying there and being unhappy wouldn't really do her justice?' He waited for someone to say, we're at *Central London Polytechnic mate, not bloody Oxford*, but nobody did.

'I think your mum sounds great.' said Ben.

And Joy added, 'Yeah me too.'

'And by the way,' Ben said looking up and grinning, 'that was the first time I have ever actually told anyone I am gay. I think that makes us bound in some way. You have to be my friends now.'

That was how it began, stumbling into the light that was adulthood and finding the tribe the swimmer had alluded to. During those first few weeks, as his new friendships blossomed, Francis phoned his mum from a call box every night. She would ask him if he was eating, and he would assure her that he was. He would ask how she was doing, and she would say that she was missing him but that was to be expected. At weekends Francis would go home, even though he wanted to stay in London with Ben and Joy, watching bands, drinking cheap wine and staying up late talking nonsense. Instead, he sat quietly at home on Saturday afternoons as Rose went about pretending he was thirteen again; offering food, suggesting things to watch on the television and worrying aloud about the bills.

'I can pay that out of my grant mum,' he said with more irritation in his voice than he wanted.

'What will you live on?'

'It's fine, I have enough.' It was a lie, but he felt relief at the thought of being the dutiful son and Rose playing the dutiful mother.

'Maybe don't come home next weekend son, it's not that I don't want to see you, but you want to be with your friends, and anyway you will save money on the train fare.'

'That makes good sense mum,' he said as he hugged her, 'and you tell me when the phone bill comes in, ok?'

*   *   *

Francis was nineteen and standing next to a girl with spiky bleached hair near the back of a small crowd in a college bar listening to a band.

'The drummer is too loud,' he said distractedly.

'The drummer is my brother,' the girl said without even checking to see if Francis had been talking to her. 'Do you like them though?'

Francis didn't want to be rude, but he didn't want to lie either, so he just stood there staring at her.

'Don't worry about it,' she said, 'I don't like them either. I'm Ana, fancy a drink?'

Two weeks later they had sex for the first time in a shared bathroom of the YWCA on Cavendish Street, where no men were allowed in after midnight. They rolled into the shower half naked at 11:40 and they were back out again, dressed and giggling by 11:49, sitting staring at each other like grateful puppies.

It had been four weeks since he had last been home, but he wanted to take Ana to meet his mum. He wanted his mum to see him happy and to show her that the life he was living could be brought to Birchington, but it could not be lived there. Afterwards he asked Rose what she thought.

'She's perfectly nice.'

'She has so much energy, Mum,' he said enthusiastically. 'She crams so much into every day, and she cares about everything.'

'She has funny hair…she could be quite pretty if she didn't put so much rubbish on it.'

After four months Francis was beginning to find Ana exhausting.

'No wonder her brother took up the drums, she doesn't stop talking.' Ben had said after they had split up. 'When she was out with us I was always thinking, kiss her Francis, kiss her now so the rest of us can get a word in.'

Francis' next girlfriend was Louise. She was doing a law degree, ran marathons and when Francis took her home for a day trip, she bought Rose flowers.

'She is clever, she can play the harp,' Francis told Rose.

'The mouth organ?'

'No, the harp; a real harp.'

'I think she's a bit stuck up, son, and she has swollen ankles. She won't make old bones.'

'Some people don't,' he muttered, and resolved to stop bringing girlfriends back to his mum.

At the end of his first year at Polytechnic Francis moved back home and got a job on the farm he used to run across to get to the sea. He liked working outdoors and the money was good. He gave Rose three quarters of what he earned and saved the rest, knowing that when he was back in London he would be able to send it home when she needed it. He would speak to Ben and Joy on the phone every week and they had asked if they could come and visit him. 'It's not much of a house,' Francis had said self-consciously, 'but you would be very welcome.'

Rose loved the idea. 'You never brought friends home when you were at school, I thought you were ashamed.'

'I didn't have friends then mum. Now I do.'

'They could have Grandad's room,' she said, 'although we burned the mattress. We could buy a new one. Can we afford that? Then you could have that room when you move back home after college?'

'If mum, if,' he said quietly.

'Does your mum think we are a couple?' Joy asked when they arrived.

'We could pretend if you like?' said Ben. 'No, you don't have to pretend anything here,' said Francis.

Rose cooked a Roast dinner and when they had finished she brought them out a home cooked apple pie.

'You've never made an apple pie in your life' Francis teased.

'I bet your mum and dad are glad to have you home?' Rose said to Ben, ignoring her son.

'They don't like me Mrs Broad. I spent some time with my Grandfather but he only has a small house and I feel that I get in his way. Coming here for a couple of days is like a holiday for me and I am very grateful, thank you.'

Rose was confused. 'What do you mean they don't like you?'

'I'm gay Mrs Broad. They are disappointed.'

'But...they are your parents.'

'Yes.'

There was a silence and then Rose said, 'I had an uncle who was a homosexual. He got beaten up by some men outside a pub in Margate once,' she sighed. 'I don't know why, he wouldn't hurt a fly. Who he loved was his business wasn't it?'

'I think you're right Mrs Broad.'

'Call me Rose,' she said with an enthusiasm that suggested to Francis that she was prepared to adopt Ben, and then looking at Joy, she said, 'and you too dear…are you a…erm…?'

'No, Mrs Broad – Rose – no I'm not.'

Rose nodded at her, but you and Francis are not…?'

'No Mrs Broad,' Joy blushed, 'we're just good friends.'

Francis was shaking his head and Ben and Joy were grinning.

'I'm glad, not that you aren't lovely, but Francis, well Francis has needed some good friends for a long time.'

*　　　　*　　　　*

By the age of twenty-three Francis had a mediocre Humanities degree, a small housing association flat in Hackney and a second-hand bicycle. He was working as a gardener in Regents Park, having first picked up work there during the holidays as a student and he just kept going back every chance he got because he enjoyed it and because having a job in London meant moving back to Birchington was out of the question. He liked watching things grow and filled with the sense of time slipping past – twenty-three was over a third of the way through his allotted time – he liked keeping a close eye on the coming and going of the seasons and imagined that it would somehow slow down time. It didn't.

By the time he was twenty-eight, he was teaching part time at a local college, which pleased Rose very much. She had given up on her son moving back home and being a teacher made better sense of him having gone away in the first place. It also seemed to her to be a more acceptable profession, in a way that gardening was not. He had got into teaching because one of the people he worked with in the park had asked him to stand in one day when he was sick.

'Just show them how to seed stuff, preferably vegetables, we are on vegetables this week.' The man had said. He was a stout, grey haired Welshman called William, who had taught Francis how to cut back the roses when he had started in the parks, and who had the cleanest hands Francis had ever seen on a person who worked with dirt. The following week he still wasn't better, in fact William never came back, he moved to Shropshire and grew award winning dahlias which Francis suspected had always been his plan.

At thirty-one Francis was still teaching part time and had gravitated from the park to working as a self-employed gardener, hiring himself out to shape, renovate or simply tidy domestic gardens; mostly tending to the gardens of people who were either too busy, too frail, or too bored by plants to do it themselves. On the weekends he would see Ben and Joy to catch up on what they had been doing – building things from wood and playing music for money respectively – and who they were seeing – pretty, enthusiastic, flawed men in both cases – and they would eat and drink or howl at the moon together. Time was still passing quickly but for a little while at least he had learned to ignore it.

Francis liked his work but sometimes, as an antidote to the mud, he would go swimming in the ponds at Hampstead Health. He would cycle home thinking about the sea, how he missed its vastness and its movement and he would try to remember how it tasted, how it made his skin smell for hours after he had got out. He never felt this at the ponds, yes, he could swim there but they were often crowded, and it was difficult for him to get into his stroke. Sometimes Ben and Joy would join him there, Joy wearing a bobble hat and shivering as she stood waist high in the water, Ben laying on his back, looking up at the sky and kicking his legs.

'It's alright once you're in, isn't it?' Joy would shout to him in a high-pitched voice across the lanes of swimmers.

'It is,' he would say. 'but it's not as good as the sea.'

One evening, as he cycled home from the ponds, along the Essex Road in Islington, a Ford Sierra decided to turn right regardless of Francis and it hit him hard, spinning him up into the air and across the roof of the car like a wave crashing over a harbour wall. As he bounced from the car roof two things went through his mind. The first was; I need to land well, and the second was, I'm thirty-two, I haven't finished with my allotted time yet.

Francis initially thought he had landed well, but he hadn't considered the added momentum the car had lent him and after rolling on to his feet he kept crashing forward, eventually hitting the road with his shoulder, then his head, and then his ribs. His bike didn't land well at all, it went under the car and buckled in two. When the terrified looking man who had been driving the Sierra ran over to him, close to tears and asking if he was alive, Francis rubbed his head and said 'Don't worry, I'm ok, how are you, that must feel awful, hitting someone with a car, sit down with me if you like.'

Then Francis passed out.

He was taken to hospital with a suspected concussion, a dislocated shoulder and three broken ribs. He was kept in overnight for observation and later the following day he was discharged with pain killers and his arm in a sling. He got a taxi to his flat in Hackney and sat quietly with a cup of tea. Ben was there to see him within the hour with fruit and groceries gathered from a local shop and half a bottle of Jack Daniels gathered from his kitchen.

'You smell of varnish.' Francis said.

'You say that like it's a bad thing. You ok?'

'Pissed off that I don't have a bike now,'

'We can get another, and this time maybe a helmet?'

They drank tea, staring out of the window at nothing more than the building opposite

'Joy will be over tomorrow, she's in Birmingham recording something with someone quite well known who I have never heard of. She'll bring cake.' Ben said.

Francis nodded but didn't speak.

'What's up?' Ben asked.

'I just drift really.'

'Don't we all?'

'You don't, not really.'

'There's no difference between you and I.'

'There is though. You have wood.'

Sometimes when they were together at weekends Francis had watched as Ben worked in silence; no radio, no distraction, no conversation, wholly lost in the task at hand. Ben would breath life into the pieces of wood and people paid a lot of money for what he made.

That is true, I do have wood,' said Ben, ' but you grow the wood, I think, do you plant trees?' I don't know what you plant. Flowers, I know you plant flowers.' Ben was smiling, trying to draw some of the misery from his friend.

'Yes, I plant trees. But it will be years before they are big enough for you to turn them into tables, you vandal.'

'I can wait. But really… what's up? Do you feel like you had a near death experience? Because, you know, you probably did.'

'I'm too young to die,' Francis said, 'but I'm not really doing anything with my life am I?'

'How do we know if we are doing anything?'

'You know, don't you? You have found something you love...you love making stuff.'

'Don't you love growing stuff?'

'It's not the same. I feel like I'm missing something, like I should be living...more...I should be living more than I am, doing more, feeling more, fitting more in.'

'Why?

For the first time in his life Francis felt an urge to tell someone about the swimmer, about his contract and the incessant rush of time slipping past, but he worried that he would sound mad, or worse, that he might somehow breach the contract and Rose would become ill again. *Secrets are a barrier to the world*, he thought.

'I don't know...just forget it...It is probably the drugs,' Francis said, 'do you want some?'

*   *   *

After the accident the college had sent Francis flowers that he and the students had grown. He was touched and when he returned to work he went to the office and thanked the secretary for them.

'We were going to send chocolates,' she said, 'it was Ms Cummings, the new Deputy Principal's, idea to send the flowers. She said it was more thoughtful.'

'Nice choice,' he said and made a note to look out for Ms Cummings.

He met her two weeks later during a tea break at a staff development day.

Victoria Cummings was standing on her own and Francis thought she looked lonely or at least alone and self-conscious. The rest of the staff were either upstairs on the roof terrace smoking or huddled round the biscuits, unsure or afraid to talk to the new College Deputy Principal. Francis retained a sympathetic eye for the outsider and he saw one in Victoria Cummings, not least because she was so near the door that she was very close to actually being outside. She had been at the college for two months, and nobody knew very much about her apparently. Consequently it had been said that she was married to a Frenchman who didn't like being in England, she was single and moved to Hackney from Camberwell after a broken relationship, was a lesbian who owned six cats, or she had no experience of further education at all and had slept her way to the top – the funniest part of which was the idea that working in a run-down technical college in Hackney was the top. All Francis saw was a woman with long hair, big eyes and wearing a million bangles on her wrist standing alone in a room full of people, so he wandered over to her.

'Hi, I'm Francis,' he said, 'what sort of music do you like?'

She laughed, 'Is this a test?'

'Well, it might turn into one if you say Queen or something, but I don't want to ask you about the upcoming presentation and it's not my place to offer you a biscuit…'

'Queen,' she deadpanned.

'You know where the biscuits are.'

'What do you teach?'

'Horticulture, part time. I'm the person who got knocked off his bike and instead of getting sent chocolates got sent flowers I had grown myself.'

'We had a collection and I kept the money. Education is a cutthroat business.'

'So, what's your favourite Queen song then? Is it the long one about the Scaramouche. What is a Scaramouche? I think it's some sort of lizard?'

She nearly spat out the sip of tea she was just taking and said, 'I'm actually a Smiths fan. Everything else pales. I saw The Bad Seeds on Saturday at the Apollo and they were very good. How am I doing?'

'Better than your predecessor, he liked The Rolling Stones, no wonder we killed him.'

'Music for people who don't really like music,' she smiled.

'Exactly,' beamed Francis.

If Francis had felt self-conscious about the burgeoning friendship that followed – occasional lunches together, chats over coffee and after a few months shared trips to see bands or plays – it passed quite quickly, and perhaps surprisingly, nobody who worked at the college commented on their relationship. There was an initial flurry of gossip but after a while this died down, people just assumed they were friends who occasionally went out together, and this is how it felt to Francis too. He liked her, of course, she was friendly to everyone, friendly but always professional and when he was with her he felt that he was more patient, less earnest and a more thoughtful person.

One evening after they had gone to see Night Of The Iguana, which had left them with the impression that it was warmer than it was, they chose to sit outside on the South Bank, feeling cold and pretending to themselves that the Thames looked nice.

'Why don't you have a boyfriend?' Francis asked.

'I don't know.' Victoria said. 'You tell me?'

'How would I know?'

'Well, you're a boy.'

'Yes, but I am not all of the boys.'

'No but you see me as a friend. We hang out, we talk, what stops that being anything else?' She blushed as she said it, and Francis blushed too. He may also have shrugged.

'How many people have you seen since we have been friends?' She asked.

'It depends, what you mean by seen,' Francis said defensively.

'Well, I'm not conducting an audit but you and I speak most days, go to gigs or the cinema and I wonder if you have ever thought about kissing me? I may be the sort of woman men think of as sisterly. I sometimes wonder if I exist to keep you company while you look for a wife.'

'I don't believe in marriage,' Francis said.

'Right.'

'Well, I believe in it in so far as it exists, but I don't really approve of it. It's on my list; horses, kebabs, guns, actors who make records...I could show you the list.'

'I'm being serious.'

'Well maybe we have more to lose. I mean if we accidentally slept together, and it didn't work out and we couldn't be friends, that would be a loss wouldn't it.'

'Ok,' said Victoria raising her eyebrows, 'first, people don't accidentally sleep together. Not really. And second you are sounding like one of those men who can't speak about their feelings clearly and I never took you for that.'

'We work together. I think there is an unspoken rule

around that, don't you think?'

'Twat.'

Francis leaned across the table and kissed her. He felt her tooth collide with his upper lip and he tasted gin, but she smiled anyway, and he liked that.

They went back to her basement flat and made love like two people trying to put on the same duffel coat in the dark, but afterwards neither of them were sad, and so they did it again.

*   *   *

Francis was thirty-three and he and Victoria had been together for nearly five months. It was his longest relationship, so he offered to resign and look for another job.

'Why?' asked Victoria.

'Well because you are the Deputy Principal, and I am mainly just a gardener.'

'Is it a bit like Lady Chatterley's Lover?'

'Not remotely.' Francis sighed, 'It's just, I don't know...' He didn't really know what it was he was trying to be sensitive about but something about Victoria made him want to try harder to be nice.

'Do you want to look for another job?'

'Not immediately.'

'But...?'

'I miss the sea.'

Francis could feel her waiting for him to say more. When he didn't she said, 'Why don't we go to the seaside for the weekend then?'

'We could go swimming whilst we are there.' Francis said.

'No we couldn't, but you could.'

'Why not you?'

'First, it is March, and second, I can't swim.'

'You can't swim? Why wasn't I informed of this?'

'It didn't come up on the girlfriend questionnaire.'

'Well, I'll have to look into that for next time,' he said, 'but in the meantime, I could teach you.'

'I am willing to give it a go, however that go will not be in the English Channel in winter, you utter madman.'

'It's virtually Spring…'

'No it isn't.'

As it was, neither of them swam. It rained all weekend and they trudged along Brighton seafront, ate chips under a leaky shelter on the pier, got cold wet feet and spent the afternoon in bed in a small hotel on Regency Square. When they got up Francis drew back the heavy curtains, made tea and pulled two chairs to the window where they could sit and look at the sea. The windows were wet with rain, the sky was grey and the sea merged into it until it rolled into the brown pebbled beach where slow white waves toppled over, exhausted and spent.

'Are you sure you can't swim?' asked Francis.

'Pretty sure. For what it's worth though, I could live here, or somewhere else by the sea.'

'Me too,' smiled Francis. 'Might take a while though?'

'No rush,' said Victoria. 'We're still young.'

'Speak for yourself. And we should try to have a baby,' said Francis with no idea where those words had come from.

'Try what?'

'A baby, we should have a baby.'

'You make it sound like giving a new restaurant a go.'

'No I don't, you're just being defensive.'

Until that moment, when the words had surprised him as much as her, Francis had not given any conscious thought to being a father. He waited for some part of him to say sorry, that it was too quick, too ridiculous, but instead he bit his lip and noticed that he felt quite excited. He glanced at Victoria who was staring at him.

'And what if we succeeded?'

'Well, what an adventure that would be.'

'Wait, are we moving to Brighton or having a baby first?' Victoria giggled.

'We can multi-task.'

'I would like to have a baby,' Victoria said as if she were revealing a secret she had never told a soul, and Francis ran his finger down her arm. 'I would like to have your baby,' she whispered.

11

Rae was conceived on the Greek Island of Spetse. Francis
and Victoria had planned to spend a fortnight there splitting
their time between the small sandy beaches and the fresh
green hills, but two days before they arrived those hills
caught fire. The centre of the island had been turned into a
black smouldering dust which made the air taste of ash and
burnt olives, so Francis and Victoria spent more time in the
apartment than they had planned for.

This was their first holiday together, and it was at once
romantic and playful but also an experiment in togetherness;
trying on partnership like a new pair of shoes and seeing how
they felt. Francis would get up early each day, whilst Victoria
dozed in bed, and head to the thin shingled beach for a swim
in the clear warm water. On the way back to the apartment he
would buy fresh bread, cheese, and fruit juice and he would
find Victoria sitting on the balcony in a sun hat, reading
when he returned. Before they ate they would go back to bed
and make love again. They were enacting a tacit, unspoken
agreement. *Now is the time, let's dare ourselves to make a baby.*

In the afternoons they would go to the beach together and on one day Francis even managed to coax Victoria into the water, but as soon as she was up to her waist, she became tense.

'You can't swim because you are as stiff as a board,' he said, 'just lay back in the water, I will hold you.'

She would try leaning back but to Francis it felt as though he had just invited her to lie back in the mouth of a shark.

'Relax, the water has you, and I have you too.'

'This is me relaxed.'

'I think you have trust issues,' he said, as he lay underneath her, letting her body rest partly on his, her head on his chest. 'Just breath.'

'You are in charge of teaching our children how to swim,' she said, standing up again, 'I really don't enjoy being at the mercy of the kraken or crabs or giant squids.'

'Children?' Francis smiled. 'Plural? Interesting.'

'Right, I'm getting out, I'm all wet.'

Victoria returned to her book and lay back elegantly on the lounger as Francis swam and thought about how different they were and how much he liked that.

That evening they wandered down a long steep hill and had dinner and drank wine in a taverna by the sea.

'I would love to live here one day,' said Francis. 'Not necessarily on this Island but on a Greek Island, a quiet one. Maybe learn how to build a garden here, in this heat.'

'I thought we were going to live in Brighton?'

'We are, but after that we can live here.'

'For a man who doesn't give the impression of planning ahead, you do plan ahead.'

'Do you like it here though?'

'I do, I think it is beautiful, but then I may also be a

little drunk?'

'Like that is a bad thing.'

Two weeks after they had returned from Spetse they found themselves sitting on the living room floor of Victoria's flat. It was three days after her period was due and they were both staring at the pregnancy testing kit that lay unopened on the floor in front of them.

'What do you think?' Francis asked.

'I don't know, I don't feel different. At least I don't think I do.'

'What would we do?'

'What do you mean what would we do?'

'Where would we live? How would we live?'

'We should live together, I think?'

'We should, definitely,' said Francis coyly. 'It would make more sense.'

'You old romantic,' she mocked.

'In your own time then.' Francis nudged her and nodded at the testing kit.

Victoria leant back into him and didn't move. It occurred to Francis that she was hesitating because she didn't want to find out that she was not pregnant; that this moment was worth staying in if only because the next one, the one that said she was not going to have a baby, would hurt more than she had imagined.

'We would make a great family,' he whispered.

'What if it's negative?'

'We keep trying, trying is fun too.'

She sighed, 'I need a wee.'

When she came back they didn't look at the plastic stick, they just sat there holding hands until Francis said, 'We should definitely move to Brighton.'

'One thing at a time,' she said, pointing at the stick.

Francis picked it up and they looked at it together.

'Fucking hell, I'm pregnant.'

Francis put his arms round her and found himself thinking vaguely about his own father, about how irrelevant he had chosen to be and how easy it had been for him to drift away from his wife and his son. Becoming a father was reasonably straightforward if the bodies and the gods aligned. Being any good at it demanded some concentration, some effort, some attention, and it required staying present, no matter what. He vowed that all of the things his own father had failed at, he would not.

Victoria buried her face into Francis's chest so he could not see her face, she had no idea as to what sort of mother she might become. There was a revolution beginning beneath her skin, a collection of cells gathering deep inside her that were unique and dependent on her and as they sat on the floor, hugging each other, the world slowly changed colour.

'I will be the best of dads,' Francis said as he kissed Victoria on the top of her head.

'I know,' she said, without looking at him 'That's why I chose you.'

Four weeks later Francis and Victoria drove down to Birchington to tell Rose the news. Francis had wanted to tell her on the phone but the ever-cautious Victoria had told him to wait until she had seen a doctor, had the pregnancy confirmed and taken some time to let the new reality settle in. On the way the windscreen wipers of Victoria's classic Triumph Herald stopped working and the car shook with disapproval every time they went over sixty-five mph.

'We will need a different car, a sensible one,' said Francis. 'Not too sensible, but safe, certainly safe.'

'A tank maybe?' offered Francis. 'A small one, easy to park.'

Rose was slimmer now; she had collected tiredness around her eyes and even though Francis saw her every two months or so he felt she looked two years older every time. The withering of Rose was not something he had imagined, nor was it something he was able to prevent, but he watched it and felt a pang of guilt every time he saw her. Except today. Today was different.

'Any news?' he asked as soon as she opened the door.

Rose stood up, hugged him and before she could respond Francis said, 'Ok, we'll go first. Victoria is carrying your grandchild, now your turn...'

Rose stared at him and Francis imagined that she had begun to turn from the faded grey she had been inhabiting to something approaching technicolour. Then she began to cry. She said it was with joy, and when she put her arms round Victoria she did it with something approaching reverence.

'I never thought I would be a grandmother...'

'I never thought I'd be a mum,' whispered Victoria, which as far as Rose was concerned bound them together forever.

*   *   *

They were sitting on the roof terrace of Ben's new apartment in Camden, overlooking the canal. It was a warm autumnal day, and the water was so green that it didn't cross Francis's mind to swim in it. They could see two children on a houseboat feeding the ducks and the only noise was the wind in the trees.

'How is pregnancy?' Ben asked.

'This is the first time in over a week I have felt able to leave the flat,' offered a pale and tired Victoria, 'I have been invaded by a body snatcher.'

As much as Victoria wanted to love pregnancy, it simply didn't love her back. From the first trimester she had morning sickness, haemorrhoids, painful breasts and hypertension. Francis thought she looked wonderful and said so, which didn't help. She felt tired all the time and she cried often and randomly. She had been determined to relish growing a child, to notice her body doing what her body did and to remember that billions of women had done this before her and billions more would do it after, but she was finding it harder and harder to love what was happening to her. At the twenty-week scan she was diagnosed with preeclampsia. The nurse who began their appointment warm and chatty grew quieter, more pensive and had told them that although the baby was doing fine Victoria's blood pressure was quite high. The nurse then excused herself and returned with a doctor who barely acknowledged Francis. After prodding Victoria's ankles, asking her about how often her morning sickness stretched into the afternoon and whether she had any blurred vision, the doctor told Victoria she had preeclampsia and that the hospital needed to keep a closer eye on her to make sure that she and her baby were going to be alright.

'You should have told me how you were feeling, I could have come to your place and saved you the hassle of coming over here,' said Ben as he reached out and gently squeezed her hand.

'It's good to be out, really. Although, I may need to go for a little lie down, just to get my energy back.'

'Come on,' said Ben, 'have a rest, lay on my bed, and please excuse the mess.'

Ben led Victoria through his flat and after she had settled he returned to the balcony carrying two bottles of beer.

'The poor love,' he said as he handed a beer to Francis, 'I can't help feeling that if there was a God, and he or she had any sense of justice, they would find a way to share the pain a bit, after all, you are going to be a dad, at the very least your nipples should really hurt.'

Francis laughed. 'Speaking of God, will you be godfather? Well, you know, whatever the equivalent of godfather is for someone who doesn't have a God.' Ben looked as if he were going to cry.

'Oh Francis...that's amazing... I would love that. Thank you, thank you so much...what do you need me to do?'

'Care, I think? Maybe help fill in some of the gaps I will inevitably leave. Wood for example, if the baby wants to know about what happens to the trees I grow after they are brutally chopped down you might step in?'

'Right, so basically provide guidance on all the things you know nothing about?'

'Yeah.'

'That's a lot of stuff to cover, how many godfathers are you planning to have?'

'Just you,' said Francis. 'And we are going to ask Joy to be godmother.'

'Well, I'm honoured, really, and I will start by making the baby something.'

'No need...'

Ben shook his head 'I need to make the baby something beautiful.'

'ok, but to be honest, I was hoping for some babysitting.'

'I can do that, too.'

The rest of the pregnancy felt to Victoria like a physical assault by surrealist plumbers. Her private relationship with her baby became a spectator sport. She was prodded and probed, talked about and medicated. Francis practiced helplessness and stopped sleeping. Rose would phone him and say; 'babies do not come easy to us, son, but they come.' Which comforted him for as long as an echo. Everything in him was reduced to outsider, he hovered around Victoria like a hungry gull.

'I'm scared,' Victoria would say.

'I am too, we're scared together. No matter what.' And he meant it. Deep down, beneath his powerlessness, he felt that if he stopped concentrating on her and the baby and the invisible web that connected them, everything would fall apart. So, he stayed as close as she could bear and at night, when she was asleep and he lay beside her, keeping guard, he found himself thinking about the swimmer. What would he offer to keep Victoria and their baby safe, what would he be willing to give to reduce her pain now, how many years would he give away to keep them all safe? What would that sacrifice mean, would his absence when his child turned five, or ten or fifteen be any different to that of his own father's?

*   *   *

When Rae was two weeks old, Ben and Joy drew up outside Victoria's basement flat, which Francis had by then moved in to. Francis and Victoria – who was holding the crying Rae and bouncing her lightly up and down on the off chance she wanted to sleep – watched from the window as Ben carefully carried a rocking chair down the steps and rang the bell.

'I made this for you,' he said as he brought the chair carefully into the living room and put it down where Victoria had been standing. 'Here all right?'

'It's beautiful,' Francis said.

'He is very proud of this,' said Joy as she kissed Francis on the cheek. Then she kissed Victoria and said, 'may I?' as she put her arms out to take the baby.

Victoria handed Rae over and said, 'she's tired but won't sleep, don't take it personally if she starts screaming in a minute.'

'I can't make chairs,' Joy said with a wink to Victoria, 'but I'll always hold your baby for you if you need me to.'

'I started this the day after you came round and weren't feeling well,' Ben said. 'I got the wood from a tree in Springfield Park that came down in a storm. The council were cutting it up and I thought it was such a lovely texture I could make something good from it. The tree fell over so think of this as its resurrection. I wanted you to have something...to have this.'

'I don't know what to say,' Victoria was crying again. 'Bloody hormones. Thank you, thank you very much.' And when she turned to look at Rae, who was fast asleep in Joy's arms, it made her cry a little bit more. 'I have never thought of myself as someone who cries before,' she said.

'My mum had a difficult birth with me,' said Joy. 'She said that afterwards it took a while to, and I quote, get back on an even keel. It makes sense I think, you have been through a storm, tossed around by this beautiful, beautiful tempest that grew inside of you but the keel will keep the ship steady and the storm will calm itself eventually. All storms do.' Joy handed the sleeping baby back to Victoria and added quietly,

'Oh, and we brought cake.'

Francis had to go back to work two weeks after Rae was born, but when he was there he thought about Rae nearly all of the time. She was the most remarkable thing he had ever seen, she smiled, cried, blinked, picked things up, often accidentally, only to be surprised to find herself holding a pen or a toy or her own foot and not knowing how to put it down again. He could watch her do this for hours. He worked happily and hard grinning while he dug. He was currently renovating a large walled garden to a detached house for a retired GP whose daughter had moved to California and taken her two grandsons with her.

'I could go there of course,' she told Francis over a cup of tea one afternoon, 'but I feel as though I belong here still? I'm me here, whatever that means, if I go there I become someone else, a former me, does that make sense?'

'Maybe that is why you are doing your garden?'

'How do you mean?'

'Gardens,' he hesitated, 'gardens hold us to a place, I think? When we make them we make a sort of...a commitment. It's not that we can't break that commitment of course, you can divorce a garden but few people who have taken the time to make one let it go without thinking about it.'

'It's not just about making a prettier space then.' The woman stared at him. 'So, what sort of tree do you think I need to plant in that barren corner, and is there enough room?'

'Plenty of room, Francis said. 'What you could do is have a couple of fruit trees, small ones, you could espalier them, that is tie them to some wires and train them so they grow along the wall at the back there, it gets sun, they will look lovely and dare I say hide that wall quite nicely. And you will get fruit.'

'What fruit?'

'Whatever you like really, apple, plum, pear, cherry.'

'How about two apples and a plum, the apples for my grandsons and the plum for your daughter.'

'What a wonderful idea,' Francis beamed.

After planting those first fruit trees he decided to try to plant as many as he could, for Rae. He would make a note of what and where they were and when she was bigger he would drive past the houses and show them to her. It was possible that at seven she might be charmed by the idea and at fourteen appalled by how ridiculous her gardening father was, *but,* he reasoned, *when I'm not here, there will still be the trees.*

One day when he was working at the college Victoria had phoned him and he had instinctively worried that something was wrong, but she just needed to tell him that Rae had turned over, on her own, and that she had done it again to prove it wasn't an accident.

'I filmed it for you,' she said.

When Francis watched it, he thought it was the most wonderful thing he had ever seen. That night, like the other nights he slept lightly, listening out for Rae, standing guard over his family. If she woke, he would leap from bed and go to her, stroking her head, shushing her, staring at her. He had spent all his life trying to make his world larger; looking outward as far as he could, always wondering what it would be like to be somewhere else. Now the world was no bigger than the space between Victoria, Rae and him and he was happier than he had ever been. Once Rae had settled again, he would creep quietly back to bed. Victoria would be close to sleep, eyes pressed tightly shut, she would reach out her hand and pat him wordlessly by way of saying thanks, well done, go back to sleep, don't speak to me. But even when she slept she looked as though her body still ached.

'Why am I still so tired?' Victoria would ask in the morning, before Francis went to work.

'Because you grew a person, and you are only little, stop being so hard on yourself.'

Sometimes when, he came home from work she would immediately hand him Rae and slump down onto the sofa.

'I'm sorry,' she would say, without looking at him. 'I just need twenty minutes.' He would take Rae out for a walk, feed the ducks in the local park, point at the flowers, and hope that Vic would rest. But when he got back he found a tidy house, dinner nearly ready and a woman desperate to pick up her baby again, because Rae had been away for an hour and Victoria had missed her.

'Are you happy?' He would whisper to Victoria.

'I am,' she said. And she would squeeze his hand before curling into a ball and falling asleep.

'Me too,' he would say to nobody as he settled back into vigilance. His job was to help her; let her sleep, let her heal, he wanted to do this, needed to do it, it was his purpose, his responsibility. And he was grateful for it.

12

Francis was thirty-seven and Rae was two when they moved to Brighton. Rae would be thirty when he reached his allotted time and that would be alright, she would be alright, he would prepare her ahead of time, but not yet. Rae would slow down time for him by simply distracting him so completely from himself. He would watch her grow and every day he would gather around the detail that was his changing daughter.

They had bought a small, terraced house less than a mile from the sea, which had what was described by the estate agent as a patio garden but was really a high-walled concrete box. Francis had given up his position at the college in London and Victoria had secured a job as the Head of Arts and Humanities at a further education college in Brighton. She worked four days a week, earned enough to just about support them, and she loved being a mother. Francis thought she was born to it, that she was like Rose in that regard – and that regard alone – and when she attended in some way to her daughter, the rest of the world became wholly silent to her. Francis would watch her show Rae how to hold a pencil so she could draw, teach her what she was doing when she was cooking and, most comically, how to do a sit up.

'Why are you teaching our daughter to do something you have never done in your life?'

'Everyone wants their child to know more than them.'

'So, teach her French.'

'Non. Je suis don't know any French.'

'Oh well, best stick avec le sit ups then.'

When they made each other laugh, Rae laughed too which made them happy and so laughing became their currency.

'Did you just not tell me about your degree in Mumness?' he asked one evening when Rae was asleep.

'Should it be Mumness? Or Mumology? Anyway, you are just as good at Dadonomics and lets face it, you didn't have much of a teacher.'

'I think we should have five more,' he said quietly.

'We'd need a different car and I like my little Fiat.'

He told himself to be patient, *we are happy* he thought, *I am happy.*

A month later he said, 'Do you think we should try for another?'

'I want to settle into this job before I ask for maternity leave, let's not rush please?'

And so he didn't rush. Instead he set about trying to establish himself in a new city that already had plenty of gardeners. He placed adverts in shop windows and began to pick up a few jobs. His first was a brief to transform a small walled back yard into 'something with a sea theme where we can grow vegetables.' He made some raised beds, bought some pebbles, planted a baby apple tree and found some driftwood on the beach for them, which he couldn't bring himself to charge for. It was perfect they said.

'At least charge them for the time it took you to find it and carry it to their house,' Victoria told him.

'They recommended me to friends; I get more work by being nice.'

'You get more work by being cheap.'

'I'm establishing my brand..'

'Yeah, The Poundland Gardener,' she teased.

But work grew steadily, mostly by word of mouth, and he liked his life and Rae was happy, he was happy, they were all happy, and he tried not to think too much about the fact that he and Victoria hardly had sex anymore. *We're tired,* he reasoned. *And busy. And Victoria was still establishing herself in her new job. And so he turned to the sea.*

Rae turned four the year he swam right through the winter for the first time. He hadn't intended to, he simply didn't stop as the weather grew colder. As November turned in to December the sky on the seafront offered up a blank and bleak grey canvas, and every morning he would drop Rae at nursery and then walk down to the beach and slip himself into the cold and unforgiving waters.

There were often long weeks with northern winds that flattened the water, and he liked the extra chill that came with that. He would swim until he got too cold, wearing only trunks, goggles and an orange silicone cap, wanting to feel the water until all other senses left him. The water became the place to revel in his life, his contentment, his residual sense of time passing and his joy of Rae; the stories they made up, the games she played, the seriousness with which she addressed her growing world. He would get out before his body began to relish the chill too much because he knew that was the onset of hypothermia. Afterwards, he would dress quickly, drink hot tea from a flask while he stared out at the hard and silent sea and then go to work.

*   *   *

Ben and Joy were coming for the weekend. Rae was very excited and had decided it was important to dress appropriately to greet them.

'Who is Auntie Joy's favourite Princess?' she had asked Francis.

'You, definitely.'

Rae chose to wear some sparkling sandals along with combat trousers, a plastic tiara and a stripy T shirt with the words *I've Got This* written on it. When they arrived she hugged them both and waited for Joy to notice the way she was dressed which she did almost immediately.

'You look great Rae-Rae, just like a ninja princess.'

'What is a ninja princess?'

'A beautiful and very cool hero.'

Only Joy and Ben called her Rae-Rae. Victoria didn't really like the name but Rae did, it marked her out as special to them and with no natural uncles or aunts she liked having people who were special.

'We have gifts!' Ben said, 'not for your parents obviously, well wine, we have wine for your parents but for you we have…' He handed her a box. Rae opened it and inside was a finely sculpted whale shaped out of olive wood.

'Thank you Uncle Ben,' Rae gasped as she hugged him.

'You are very welcome Rae-Rae, it can't swim I'm afraid but there is not another one like it in the whole world.'

'Even under the sea?'

'Especially under the sea.'

'And from me...' said Joy, 'your parents are going to love me for this...your first piano. Later I will teach you your first song,' and noticing the expression on Francis' face, she turned to him and said, 'there is a little socket for headphones. I will tell you where it is if you bring me wine.'

Ben, Francis and Victoria were all sitting in the garden. Rae was indoors with Joy playing with the toy piano. Joy had been showing her how to play *Twinkle Twinkle Little Star* and now they had moved on to *Take A Chance On Me*, which mostly seemed to consist of two notes and lots of singing.

When Joy and Rae re-joined them, Victoria told Rae it was time to get ready for bed and after a lot of protest managed to get Rae to head upstairs to get changed, promising her she could come back down to say goodnight to everyone.

'When will she get a brother or sister, we want more non-god children.' Ben asked after they had gone.

'Surely it's one of you two to take a turn next?'

'Carlos doesn't have a womb,' said Ben. Carlos was his boyfriend, a tall, unnervingly thin Colombian model who had commissioned a bed from Ben and persuaded him to lay on it with him when it was delivered.

'I have never stayed in a relationship with anyone for more than a year.' Joy said. 'It's like I imagine the warranty is going to run out and I take them back to the shop.

'Well, you don't have to do it the conventional way,' Francis said, 'with a partner.'

Joy frowned. 'I know that,' she said, but the truth is I like visiting children, I couldn't possibly take one with me everywhere I went. I don't have a big enough bag. It's down to you Francis, to provide us with small people to buy things for and to play with.'

'I think I would make a good dad,' Ben said quietly, as if he were almost surprising himself. 'Better than mine was at any rate.'

'Surrogacy is a thing,' Francis said.

'Hire some poor stranger to carry a child? That doesn't seem morally...' he paused and looked at the sky for a moment, 'appropriate.'

Rae came running down the side passage of the house shouting 'cake, mummy has cake.' She jumped on to Ben's lap, facing Joy, reaching her hand out to her and grinning shyly. Francis watched and wondered if he could ever be happier than he was right then.

'If we are going to try for another child, we should try soon Vic.' Francis said after their guests had gone and Rae was asleep in bed.

'I know...are you doing the supermarket shop tomorrow because we need some more floor cleaner.'

'Do you want another child?' Francis asked as gently as he could.

'Yes of course I do...'

'But?'

'I don't think I can go through it again. I'm older now, not as strong.'

Francis felt a pang of something that surprised him. Anger? Impatience? He tried to swallow it down but failed.

'What is it you can't go through? The sex? The pregnancy? The joy?'

'It's not about you,' she snapped.

'I didn't think it was,' he said, 'but I am involved.'

The small living room began to feel smaller. The television flickered silently in the corner with the sound down. They both stared at it anyway, not looking at each other as they spoke.

'It's not just us, is it? There is Rae to think about too. She might not want to be an only child.'

'And what if another pregnancy kills me, what if I get through it but our baby is disabled or I am, what would that be like for our daughter? What we have is beautiful, perfect; why would we risk that?'

'Are we meant to be so grateful for one child that we can't want another?'

'We can want all sorts of things,' Victoria said, 'but that doesn't mean chasing after them is the right thing to do.'

'We could get some advice at least. Go and see someone, ask what the risks are?'

'We could,' but her tone suggested she wouldn't.

'Are we not having sex because you are scared of getting pregnant?'

'It takes two people to not have sex, Francis.'

'You don't want to try, do you?'

'Are we still talking about sex?'

'For a baby.'

'No. No, I don't.'

'Why didn't you say that before then?'

'Because I want to want to have another, and I have waited in the hope that this…this terror would go away but it hasn't. My head wants Rae to have a baby sister or brother.' She began crying. 'But I…this…' she slapped herself on the chest, 'can't. When I even think about it I get breathless, my stomach tightens, I begin to feel panic. It's like my body…my body is warning me…telling me what I can't do. What it won't do. What I am failing to do…failing you, her, and me. I feel so…I feel so separate from my own womb, my own skin, it's like it isn't even mine…' She was sobbing now, it was as if she had burst. She slid onto the floor from the sofa, holding her hair so tightly that Francis thought she was going to pull it out. He slipped down beside her, so his shoulder was just touching hers and stayed like that as she cried. After a few minutes, as she began to run out of breath, he put his arm round her shoulder and stroked her back until she let go of her hair.

'I'm sorry,' he whispered. 'I didn't realise, I mean I knew but…I didn't know it felt this hard. We are so lucky, Vic, so very lucky. What sort of greedy bastard asks for more than this?'

He felt a thin, stinging sadness spreading through him. Some of it was hers, leaking into his skin as he rested against her, but most of it was his own, rising from the pit of his stomach and spreading across his chest. But it was mixed in with something else, something that he tried to ignore and could not or would not have named, something unsettling and heavy that was putting roots down. It might be anger, he thought, or shame or just simply an overwhelming, heart-breaking disappointment.

When they went to bed they were silent. Victoria curled up tightly and seemed to go to sleep straight away but Francis knew she was awake. He lay quietly staring at the ceiling. Rae was the only child of two only children, Rose used to tell him that he had held on to life so tightly as a baby that his tiny fingers could have fallen off and he had imagined clinging to a rock in the middle of the sea during a storm, desperately trying not to sink to the bottom of the ocean, determined to exist and forever grateful for being allowed to. Victoria had fought just as hard for their daughter. Every day of her pregnancy she was holding on to the thing that was setting fire to her from the inside and despite that, when she was born, she loved her with every ounce of her being. *Babies don't come easy to us son, but they do come.* That is what Rose had said, and Francis wondered why the world was so reluctant to welcome him and his babies to the planet.

The following weekend, they took Rae to the park and watched as she chased the pigeons.

'What will we do if she catches one?'

'Adopt it?'

'I don't want to adopt either, Francis,' Victoria said quickly.

'Blimey Vic, it was a joke, about pigeons.'

Later, in the darkness of the bedroom, Victoria reached over and stroked her husband's leg. Tentatively they touched hands, he ran his fingers down her body, she was warm and he was uncertain. Carefully, slowly, they made love. Afterwards, both of them were sad.

*   *   *

Francis was forty-two. It was late April, the days were getting longer, and even though the air still felt cool, particularly in the early mornings when Francis swam, everything seemed cleaner, brighter, made fuller somehow by the promise of spring. Nearly two years had passed since Victoria had sobbed on the living room floor, Rae had begun piano lessons and they had bought a kitten. Victoria had been promoted, Francis had started teaching again, two days a week at a local college that backed on to the Sussex Downs. He grew vegetables in the raised beds in their small back garden and he still tried to persuade the people who he did gardening for to plant a fruit tree.

When Francis arrived at the flat in Camden he sat out on the roof terrace with Ben and Joy. Ben brough them out some drinks, hugged Francis and handed him a single piece of wood wrapped in tissue paper. It was a carved breaching dolphin on a thin wooden stand. Ben had captured it at the peak of its leap from the imagined water, twisting with its beak and fin pointing up to the sky. When Ben had last been down to visit, he had watched a TV programme about dolphins; Rae had sat beside him, cuddling up and occasionally pointing at the breaching and saying, 'Dancing dolphins, Uncle Ben.'

'Do you think your daddy does that when he swims?'

'Nooo,' she giggled, and she had snuggled further into his chest, reassured that there was another safe place to rest her head.

'It's to go with the whale,' he smiled.

'That is lovely Ben; actually, it is beautiful.'

'I know she is a bit old for wooden toys, but I wanted to make something for her.'

'He made me a ukulele,' said Joy. One of the instruments I can't play.'

'I can't make pianos, Ben said, 'or at least I don't think I can. Tell him about Germany,' Ben said.

'I just got back from Germany?' Joy teased.

'About the man boy.'

She sighed, 'So I was hired to play keyboards for a singer called Arnold,'

'Arnold who?'

'Just Arnold. He came third or something on one of those

talent shows on TV and he got this tour, just twelve gigs in Germany, Holland, Belgium. Nice work really. But anyway, he's a nice enough kid, polite, not arrogant. He has the look of a boy who is expecting to be back in the call centre within six months. He's getting pushed around a bit by the people organising things and you could see him getting a bit dizzied by it all...'

'Did he storm off?'

'I said that' said Ben, 'but no, listen.'

'He collapsed,' said Joy.

'I don't really know what that means,' said Francis.

'Hypoglycaemic.' She shrugged as if that explained everything.

'Diabetic.' Ben said just in case Francis wasn't keeping up.

'Yeah, bless him, he hadn't told anyone he was diabetic. He thought they would fire him or something and he'd stopped eating in case he got fat because everyone was hassling him. But the thing is nobody had a clue what to do. One of his people,' she mimed inverted commas in the air and raised her eyebrows as she said people, 'said he was just acting out and they should leave him where he was, which incidentally was a hotel lobby, a rubbish one too. Luckily I know a hypo when I see one. I gave him chocolate, it was no big deal but now Arnold thinks he loves me.'

'And what do we think of Arnold?' Asked Francis.

'He's cute,' said Ben.

'He's twenty-four,' said Joy.

'That is quite young,' said Ben.

'I'm not sharing my chocolate with a twenty-four-year-old,' Joy was grinning.

'Or your insulin,' Ben said standing up to get more drinks.

Joy stopped smiling. 'Or that,' she murmured.

Ben turned to go into the living room and as he did so, he bumped into the back of a chair he had built when they were at college. It was, he maintained, the worst thing he had ever made, and yet he kept it to remind him of all the things you can do wrong when you try to turn a tree into something to sit on that is not just a stump. He tripped, stumbled slightly and gave the chair a petulant kick, as though it had got in his way on purpose. Then straight away he stroked the high back tenderly, as if to apologise.

'We really should have taken dance lessons,' he said to Francis without looking at him. 'I might have ended up less clumsy.'

'Never too late,' said Francis. 'Ballet, we could do ballet.'

Later on, as they sat clutching glasses of bourbon and coke, Joy asked how Rae was doing.

'She is good.' Francis hesitated. 'She leans forward, you know? Toward the world, no matter what she is doing. I love watching that, I wonder if all children do it until they fall over or bump into something too big and get a bit scared and retreat, but so far, whatever she does, she bends toward it. I love that.'

'Being a dad suits you. Are you going to have another?'

'Like Ben and Carlos, I don't have a womb. It's a bugger.' His tone was not as light as he had intended.

'Vic found it hard,' Ben said.

'She is scared, and it's not a passing fear either. She can't contemplate going through that again; her body won't let her.'

'I remember how she was,' Joy said. 'I've never had a desire to have a baby but if I had any doubts seeing what it did to Victoria convinced me I was right.'

They sat quietly, facing the canal, sipping their drinks. Ben had a blanket over his lap and was jigging his left leg up and down.

'There are worse things than being an only child,' he said.

'There are.'

'I'd like to have been an only child, preferably to other parents. You could adopt me?'

'Tempting. What is your sister doing now by the way?'

'She sells sex for money.'

'Does she?'

'No idea, but that's what I tell people if they ask in the hope it gets back to her. I think she is in banking.'

'Same sort of thing really.'

'I know.'

'Will you stop jigging your leg up and down?'

'Sorry, can't help it; you mentioned dance classes, it made me nervous.'

Francis laughed, Ben straightened his leg and put his hand on his thigh to signal it to stop.

'Shall I make more drinks?' Joy asked.

'I'll do it,' said Ben, as he stared at his leg, 'I am quite clearly a bit restless,' and then, 'I've known you since you were eighteen Francis, from the outside it looks to me as though you are happiest being a dad. And you are a dad. To the most beautiful little girl in the world.'

'I am,' Francis said quietly.

'Maybe stop thinking so much about what you can't have, revel in what you've got? Ben said.

And Francis knew his friend was right. *Look after your family and be grateful,* he told himself. And he would, he really would, just as soon as he could stop being so angry with Victoria.

13

'I'm not very well,' Ben said to Francis two weeks later. They were sitting on the roof terrace and Ben was staring out at the trees that overhung the canal.

'In what way?'

'Parkinson's.'

'Fuck...Ben.'

'Yeah.'

'What treatment...'

Ben looked at Francis and gave the lightest of shrugs.

'Nothing very useful I'm afraid. My father would say it was God punishing me, so we won't be telling him.'

'It can develop slowly, can't it? Parkinson's? It can take years to take hold...'

'Apparently.' Ben nodded, 'Or it can move quite quickly.' He sighed and looked at his right leg which was perfectly still. 'You know when you are young and people ask what you want to be when you grow up? And you had to say something that was either ludicrous or admirable, like astronaut or radiographer or monk or teacher or whatever?'

'Yeah.'

'Well, I just wanted to be good, not just good at something although that felt really important but I mean good, in the world, good and not bad.'

Francis stared at him.

'I know it sounds ridiculous, but I had this idea in my head that if you did good things, were kind or...or...something...' he blushed, 'or thoughtful...then that would spread outward, like a bush fire. When I was young I used to close my eyes and imagine that, which is the most embarrassing thing I have ever confessed to by the way...and when my dad was such a dick, I mean such an utter, utter dick, and I came to London and was free, somehow it felt all the more important to...'

'To be good?'

'More than that. To be gracious, generous.'

'You are those things'

'I'm less ridiculous than I might have been, given my circumstances.' Ben was speaking quietly, looking down at his lap.

'You're the least ridiculous person I know.'

Ben smiled. 'It's a shame really.'

'What is?'

'That I won't have more time to practice being a good human.'

'Why do you say that?'

'I have Parkinson's, mate.' Ben looked at Francis. 'You know, I am trying to finish a cabinet that would usually take me ten days. It has been nearly three weeks so far.'

'Are there drugs that help?'

Ben ignored the question. 'Thing is, when I work, there is this point where I touch the wood, shape it, prepare it, meet it…and that for me feels like…I don't have the words…it's like life, the moment when I am most alive, when I shape part of the world into something that will be, I hope, beautiful. And I can't live without that now.'

'So you adjust, we adjust, you learn to be slower…'

'When the time comes,' Ben continued, 'I will choose to not live rather than to live without the ability to do what I do. I'm not going to argue with my friends about it, and I am not going to argue with the State about it either.' He was looking directly at Francis now with a blank expression.

'You've already had this talk with Joy, haven't you?'

'Yes.'

'What did she say?'

'She just put her arms round me and said she knew.'

'And what do you need me to do.'

'The same.'

Francis stood up and went over to his friend, crouched down beside him and put his arms round him.

'How is Carlos taking it?'

'He took the illness better than he took my feelings about it.'

Francis stood up. 'He loves you.'

'Let's not try to make me feel too guilty about that please?'

'Fair enough,' Francis said.

Do you have secrets, Francis?'

'Probably, you?'

'I've never been in love.'

'Really?'

'No. Not in love. I have loved, but it's not the same, or so I am told.'

'Does Carlos…'

'Yes, he said to me early on, I am in love, and you are not, and I said, I love you, and he cried and said, it is not the same, and I feel I let him down. I'd like to blame my father, but I don't think it has anything to do with him, not really. I think it is me.'

'But you have been loved.'

Ben did not answer, he turned back to the trees that lined the canal and asked, 'Are you still swimming?'

'Yeah.'

'It's like it's your thing, swimming isn't it?'

It felt wrong to Francis to be talking about his life, but if they were going to do it, it needed to mean something.

'Secrets…?' Francis said, looking at his friend and then, 'I have one for you, but you will think me mad.'

'I sort of do anyway.'

'When I was a kid, my mum got cancer, I was twelve and I was scared she would die and I would end up in care. Anyway, I used to go to the beach a lot, running, I think I was lonely, and maybe other things too, and I met this old bloke who swam all the time and he used to talk to me and I didn't talk to many people and he offered me a sort of swop, not a sort of swop but an actually swop, a real swop. He said that if I was prepared to give up twenty years of my life, my mum would get better. He even drew up a contract for me to sign and I signed it. He said I would have lived to eight-five but I'd have to settle for sixty-five. After I signed it, this piece of paper the man gave to me, my mum got better. I've never told anyone that before. Not even Vic, certainly not Mum, and I don't know why I am telling you now, except…well, if I could, I would drive back home and see if the swimmer is still there, see if I could make a deal, maybe give you a few of my years?'

Ben lifted his head and looked at Francis, who was staring at him.

'How many years do you think it would cost? If we were going down this particular rabbit hole Francis? How many years would you have to give up for me? Because it's not life I need, is it? It is health. I need steady hands.' His eyes were full, and his voice was getting louder. He held up his hands.

'I don't know…I'm just telling you…'

'And how many years of your daughter, my goddaughter, not having a dad would you be prepared to sacrifice…'

It was the first time Francis had ever heard Ben raise his voice. 'Maybe you had a dream, a dream about saving your mother. I think you, like a lot of men, often good men, want to rescue people. I think that is what first drew you to Victoria, maybe to me.'

'Ben…'

'No, I'm not saying it is bad, I love you for it, but for Christ's sake you really are not all-powerful Francis…'

'I know…'

'But more importantly,' Ben was crying now, 'more importantly, how fucking dare you talk about giving away years…years of being a father to Rae, years of swimming in that bloody grubby ocean of yours…those things are so precious, so very precious…'

'Hang on, you're the one who is talking about taking your own life the moment you can't do a proper fucking dovetail joint…'

'That is different, I'm talking about choosing not to live when I cannot do what I love. You are talking about choosing not to live when the thing that means most to you, your daughter, will still need you. Don't be such a fucking martyr and don't you dare ever abandon that girl.'

'I would never…'

'Really?'

Francis had never seen Ben cry or be angry, yet here he was, making him be both.

'It feels so real though Ben. The swimmer…it is inside of me…I'm sorry.'

Ben reached out and Francis took his hand.

'How old will Rae be when you are sixty-five?'

'Nearly thirty.'

'That's fair enough.' Ben smiled, which made his face look wetter. 'She'll probably be sick of you by then, you really are quite wearing.'

'I need another drink,' Francis said.

'I want to show you something in the workshop.'

They walked down the stairs and through to the large light space where Ben was at his happiest.

'I am making this for Joy,' he pointed at a half built acoustic guitar. 'I wanted to make her two so she could choose which to play according to her mood but I am slower than I was. I don't want to rush it, I want it to be special.'

'It's beautiful, she will love it.'

'She will,' Ben smiled, 'that makes me happy.'

*   *   *

When Francis got home, he told Victoria about Ben. They were sitting at the kitchen table, drinking mint tea. Rae was in bed and the house was silent.

'Aren't there drugs they can give him?'

'They won't help though, they might slow it and that's all,

138

for Ben life is about what he makes and if he can't do that, then…'

'Will he really take his own life?'

Francis nodded.

'How will he do it?'

'It didn't seem the time to ask,' he said irritably.

'And what will you do?'

'Be his friend, of course.'

She didn't say anything, and he could feel her staring at him; worried about saying the wrong thing and trying not to cry because she didn't feel it was her place to.

'How can I help you?' she eventually said.

He shook his head and said nothing and they sat in silence for nearly an hour before Victoria, stood up, leant over and kissed him gently on the head.

'He isn't alone Francis, and neither are you.'

14

'You'll need a coat today, Rae,' Francis said to his daughter.

'Weather forecast threatens storms,' Victoria said. 'Thunderbolt and lightning…'

'Very very frightening,' giggled Rae automatically.

'I should divorce you for teaching her that,' Francis said.

'We aren't married.'

'I'm going to stop at the beach after I drop Rae off, probably won't swim in this but…you know.'

He arrived in the middle of an incoming tide. There was a swirling south westerly wind dancing across the water and it made the waves collide with each other as they rolled in. They built up as they caught the steep shelving and by the time they reached the beach they were large enough to persuade Francis not to go in. *Sometimes it is just not for swimming* he thought to himself. It was beginning to rain lightly and he watched the thick black clouds out at sea edging toward land. If he had any doubts about getting in the water, just to wash off the residue of the last few days, the threat of a storm put a stop to them.

There was a woman marching along the pebbles in front

of him in her long camouflage-pattern changing robe. *She isn't going in in this, is she?* he thought, and he watched as she walked with purpose to a wooden groyne, put her bag down, took off her robe and began to get ready to swim. He thought about wandering down and mentioning the waves or saying that the tide was coming in so the sea would get rougher or pointing at the thickening black clouds and the threat of thunder but he hesitated; coy, self-conscious. Who was he to assume expertise? She could be a channel swimmer for all he knew and he would simply appear to be one of *those men* who think they know best. Swimming was private, it was none of his business. Yet he did not walk away, and he did not stop looking at her.

The woman was in her swimming costume now, she was wearing a bobble hat and no goggles which Francis thought was a bad sign. *Sometimes people come and pilchard in the surf he thought, they just lay down where the ends of the wave wash over you on the beach, feel the cold sting but never leave the ground. Perhaps she was going to do that.*

She walked to the water's edge, paused for a few seconds and then walked forward. After half a dozen steps she was up to her thighs and a large wave caught her. She staggered backwards and fell, landing clumsily on her hands and knees.

That should persuade you to stop now, Francis thought, but it didn't.

The woman stood up slowly, turned round and half jogged forward, she was lifted up and over a large wave and found herself treading water, out of her depth, about four metres from the shore.

It was raining quite hard now and Francis could feel it sharp and cold on his face, but he wanted to watch, to make sure she got out ok, and in truth he was fascinated by what she was doing and why.

The woman began to breaststroke outward, slowly, awkwardly, stretching her neck and her bobble hat above each approaching wave as if she were trying to keep her face dry. She was about twenty-five or thirty metres out now, trying to swim beyond the shelf where the waves build. She turned and looked back at the shore, hesitated, then eased on to her back, still holding her head up to keep her hat dry but now pulling both arms simultaneously back over her head and heading further outwards. She was about fifty metres out when there was the first roll of thunder. She turned again, looking out to sea, watching for the lightning that came maybe four seconds later. It was bright and wide and it should have been a signal to her to get the hell out of the water. Instead, she floated, lifted up on waves that seemed to have become more agitated by the noise from the sky and the light that followed it.

Get out of the water. Francis glanced along the promenade in both directions but he couldn't see anyone. He instinctively began to walk toward the steps to the beach, not taking his eyes from the woman who continued to float. *Are you making a story to tell your friends? Or is this something else.* He thought of Ben. *How will you do it? Will you tell me? Not like this. Please not like this.*

The next roll of thunder felt lower, fuller, louder and the lightening came immediately afterwards and hit the water. Francis saw the woman lifted from the sea, she appeared to pause in mid-air for a moment, separated from the waves, before crashing back down into the raging water. He ran toward where she had got changed and for a moment he hesitated. He thought about that hesitation a lot over the following days and weeks. *I need to get help. She will be dead before help arrives. I have to go and get her. We could both die. I don't want to die.*

He shouted and he waved his arms. It was ridiculous. The woman in the sea was unconscious. He took his clothes off, put his goggles on and ran reluctantly toward the water. He dived under the first wave, then the second and he bobbed up to see where she was. He could not see anything and so he began to swim outward, twenty, thirty, fifty strokes, the waves were lifting him up and dropping him, he was taking on water and finding it hard to breathe. He stopped, turned around, looked back at the beach, he was over fifty metres out now and he could see a woman with a dog pointing to his left, jumping up and down. He inhaled more water, began to retch, and then as he feebly swam to his left he came across a bobble hat. It was thick wool, with green and cream stripes. Sodden. Pointless. He threw it over his shoulder. He retched again and tried to take a deep breath through his nose. When he first got into the water it was the lightning that terrified him, now he was afraid he was going to drown, fifty metres from the beach, swimming in a storm, people would think him a fool.

Then the woman appeared, perhaps ten strokes away, lying face down in the water. He put his head down, swam toward her and grabbed her shoulder to turn her round but she slipped away. He grabbed her with both hands, pushed her over, then, just as a wave arrived to help, he slapped her hard on the back, trying to push water from her lungs but also because he really didn't like her and it seemed likely she was going to kill him. She retched, so he slapped her again and she began coughing.

'Kick your legs, we need to get out, just kick your legs'

Francis shouted.

She kicked one leg, feebly and coughed again as Francis put one arm around her and started trying to swim back toward shore. He got caught by a wave and in a fit of violent coughing he lost his grip on her and she began to drift. He thrashed out and grabbed her hair, pulling her back toward him, wrapping her brown, thick hair round his hand and wrist he steadied himself and tried to focus back on the beach. It was maybe thirty or forty metres away, just the length of a nice large back garden, he thought, but the waves were getting bigger, the tide was higher and when the swell lifted him up he felt as if they would both be dragged under. He could see the woman with the dog and there were other people there now, maybe a blue light flashing on the promenade. He just needed to get over the shelf.

Twenty metres out the waves were rising to their highest, normally he would take his time, normally he would wait until there was a lull and then swim fast, jump up on to his feet, run for safety the way the swimmer had done the very first time he had seen him get out of the water all those years ago. But now he had a large drowning woman under his arm,

'We are going to have to let the wave take us in, this will hurt,' he said, and that is what he did. He saw a wave rise, put both arms around the woman to protect her head, and let it drag them five, six metres in before dumping them in the shallows and crashing down on top of them.

'Is she breathing? I don't think she is breathing?' Some men in uniforms had run forward and were dragging the woman away from the water's edge.

Francis shook his head and lifted his shoulders, he was bleeding from both legs, kneeling on all fours, desperately trying to cough the sea water out of his lungs.

'What's her name?'

A dog was barking. He heard a woman say, 'he doesn't know her, he just went in to save her.'

'She is breathing.' Someone shouted and he thought, *I'm glad someone is.* Then he was sick, sea water mostly, mixed with undigested fear and relief.

*   *   *

'You did well.' Victoria was stroking his arm

'Did I?'

'You saved someone's life.'

Francis was quiet for a moment. He didn't feel as though he had done well, rather, he felt as though something very bad had happened to him.

'I suppose.' He started to cry and he didn't know why. 'I'm sorry,' he said, embarrassed.

'It must have really shaken you up, I've been telling you for years, the sea is dangerous.'

'People are dangerous,' he said defensively and then, 'maybe you were right all along.'

Rae got up and hugged him. 'You are brave Daddy.'

He shook his head because that seemed absurd.

That night in bed he lay staring at the ceiling, practicing how to breath. When he closed his eyes he found himself back in the sea, struggling for air. He didn't feel brave. He felt other things. He felt stupid. The woman didn't say a word before they took her away in the ambulance, she looked at him blankly and then closed her eyes, not with exhaustion it seemed to him, more to block out the judgement of others.

A thank you would have been nice but perhaps she didn't feel thankful. Perhaps it had been her intention to die by lightning strike in the sea.

He reached out and lightly touched Victoria's arm. She was asleep and instinctively he withdrew it, reluctant to wake her. He lay on his side, with his back to Victoria, and thought about what he would be feeling now if he had simply run to a phone and stood on the shore. She would be dead, and he would be judged. *So you had your swimming things with you but decided not to go to the lady's assistance? Interesting choice sir.* But he knew it was not really a choice, and as he tentatively closed his eyes again, he thought, *it very rarely is.*

15

'Come and look at this. Did you come in your van? Did I tell you to come in your van?' said Ben as he kissed Francis on the cheek and ushered him into the workshop. 'You won't get them on the train, and I made these for you and that garden of yours at the college.

Leaning against the workshop wall were a series of hexagonally shaped wooden frames bound together to form a large carefully sculpted honeycomb

'I have made three different pieces so you can transport them but once they are in place, join them together and strap your fruit trees across them. You will have a twenty-foot trellis.'

'Espalier.' Francis said.

'Yeah, whatever.'

'Ben...they're remarkable, how did you do that?'

'Slowly, really, really slowly.'

'There is a fence that runs along the side, I could fix it to that, and we could have, four, five trees there eventually, we could even layer the trees, have plums low down, maybe pears trained to go above…or we can mix and match, we could do it so we could pick fruit right across this, it's fantastic, thank you so much.' He sounded like an excited child.

'You're welcome. It's my way of saying thank you for all the wood.'

'Where did you get the idea from?'

'I'm glad you asked, I read this article about a community garden, really nice idea, lots of people got together, took over some derelict land and started growing things. It's in New York somewhere, can't remember exactly where but in the city, in a bit where the poor people live. Or used to live. They were going to turn it into luxury apartments but one of the locals was a designer or something and they got a local college involved and so it became this, well, space. They have trees, strapped to trellises like these round the sides, and they have beds for vegetables and lots of flowers and there are slopes that they use as a design feature, and paths and some people have used recycled materials to make, I don't know how to describe them, sculptures, maybe, small installations. And the trellis looked like this and I was really interested in how they did it and couldn't work it out, so I started messing around and you know me, I got a bit obsessive and came up with these. You should go and see it.'

'Maybe we could go and see this garden together?' said Francis, always conscious of trying to make plans for a future with Ben in it.

Ben smiled, 'that's a lovely idea…'

'But…?'

'I think my days of transatlantic travel are behind me.'

'Why would you say that, it mostly involves sitting on a plane, it is very unlikely they will ask you to pilot.'

Ben held out both hands, they were shaking. 'I get tired Francis, and clumsy. That?' He pointed at the trellis, 'that took bloody ages.' He looked away and walked slowly out of the workshop. 'Fancy a drink?'

Later, when they were sitting with whisky and coke on the balcony Ben said, 'These drugs make me feel sick and sleepy, I think all drugs are basically just different coloured tranquilizers.'

'Probably doing more good than harm?' Francis said tentatively.

'Don't think so. Anyway, how are the girls?'

'Good, Rae will be ten next month, can you believe that?'

Ben shook his head, 'I'd like to have seen her at twenty, she could be anything, do anything.'

'She could,' Francis nodded, 'the thing about my daughter is, she hasn't found one thing that she wants to do above everything else...'

'She hasn't discovered wood yet,'

'There is that.'

'I would have loved to have been around for that. Wood is great.'

On the way home Francis phoned Joy. 'Missed you today,'

'I was there yesterday,' she said with a sigh, 'I thought you two might want a bit of time.'

'Without you? Never.'

'How was he?'

'Like a man putting his affairs in order.'

'Do you like the trellis?'

'It is gorgeous.'

'He made me a guitar, it is stunning.'

'Will you play it?'

'Oh yes.' And then, 'Francis, would you help him? If he asked you to, would you help him make it painless.'

'I don't know.'

'I don't mean run him over in a car or stab him, I mean turn the other way, make the inevitable less...less grotesque... if he begged you to.'

There was a silence between them until Francis said, 'I think it is too early.'

'So do I but...'

Francis knew what she meant.

'Come visit soon?' he said. 'Rae is desperate to see you, she wants you to teach her Life On Mars.'

Joy offered a mock laugh. 'Good choice, will do.'

'I think I would, you know? Look the other way. I just... it's too early.'

'Yeah, talk soon.' Joy said.

*   *   *

Ben took his own life a week later. He injected a large dose of insulin between his toes and was found in his workshop sitting in the imperfect rocking chair he had made twenty years before. He had left notes for Carlos, Joy and Francis. To Francis he wrote:

> Keep growing trees. I am grateful that I found you and that you have been my friend. I would also be grateful if you could help Carlos please? And look after Vic, she is so good for you; dare I say, let her look after you too. Tell Rae about me every few months, so she remembers the uncle who made the dolphin

*and the whale. I wanted to make her an octopus but
even at my best that may have been beyond me. She
is wonderful Francis, I love that you are the father to
such a beautiful soul.'*

The funeral, a humanist affair held in a crematorium
chapel in Camden, was arranged by Francis and Joy. Ben had
left instructions. 'Yes wear black and let there be flowers.' He
had said and there were many, many flowers, particularly
dahlias, which were Ben's favourite. Rose sent a wreath with
a card saying, 'I would have been proud of you if you were my
son,' which made Francis cry.

Francis read the eulogy and told the packed church that
Ben had thought about making his own coffin but given
he wanted to be cremated he was not prepared to create
something just to see it burn. 'He valued his work too much
for that,' he said, and he caught Joy's eye as he tried to smile.

'He put beautiful things into the world, which suited him I
think…because…' he wanted to say because he was beautiful
but he stopped being able to speak. He cried quietly for a
minute and then managed to say, 'I miss my friend, 'I will
always, always miss my friend.'

Ben's father did not attend the funeral, but his mother did.
She looked confused and out of place. A lot of Ben's friends
went out of their way to be kind to her, to tell her what a
wonderful man she had brought into the world, how talented
he was, how decent, how loved. Francis could not bring
himself to say a word to her. *How do you stay with a man who
forbids your son from coming home?* If he had said anything, it
would have been, *You left him long before he left you, oh, and tell
your husband he is an ignorant, pitiable bastard.* So, in memory of

Ben, who believed in the fecundity of kindness, he clutched Victoria's hand, stared at the floor and said nothing.

Joy had looked like a beautiful statue throughout; elegant and bloodless. She wore a veil; signalling to everyone there that she was not available for conversation. She sat with Francis, Rae and Victoria, holding Rae's hand and staring straight ahead. When she left the service she walked past Ben's mother without offering even the slightest glance in her direction, managing somehow to exude complete contempt.

Over the coming weeks Francis slipped unthinkingly back into his routine. From the outside he seemed like a shadow; a man mourning the loss of his friend. From the inside he felt completely disordered; like a man trying to rearrange his internal furniture and not knowing where things belonged.

'You look so sad, all of the time,' Victoria said tenderly. 'You can talk you know.'

'I know.'

'I know you miss him, we miss him too,' she would say.

And he would say, 'I do miss him. I miss him very much,' and then return to being quiet.

Two months later Joy drove down to Brighton with half of Ben's ashes in a cardboard box in the back of the car. Over the previous week Francis had pulled up a corner of their patio and dug a very deep hole. He had fed it with compost, mixed the best soil he could and bought a cherry blossom tree. Joy, Francis, Victoria and Rae went to the garden, opened the box and poured the ashes in They covered them with soil, dropped the cherry tree on top and surrounded it with earth. Then they watered it.

'How tall will it grow?' Joy asked

'As tall as we let it, in three years' time this will look beautiful.'

They were silent for a while, looking at the tree, feeling the sun as it began to warm the air.

'I gave him the insulin.' Joy said when Vic and Rae had gone back inside.

'I know.'

'Did he tell you?'

'He didn't need to. When did you give it to him?'

'Right at the beginning, when he told me…told us.'

'He told me that you were the best of us…'

'We both know that was never true.'

'Do we?'

'Thing is, I feel…then, when he told me it felt like, it felt like the right thing to do. It felt like I was being kind, supportive, showing him that I understood…that I had his back. Later I even wondered if, sub consciously, I was showing him…love. I always felt that was part of what we did for him, maybe for each other, you know? But now…now I feel as though I did a terrible, terrible thing, that he would be here now…'

'Or he would have found another way, an uglier, more painful, riskier way?'

'Riskier?'

'He could have tried something and failed, been disabled, lost his hands, lost even more power over his own life, that would have been torture for Ben, you know that. Or he could have died in agony, I pulled someone from the sea Joy and I thought of Ben afterwards, drowning, jumping under a train, falling from a cliff…there are some bloody awful ways to die.'

'I remember Ben always used to laugh with me when we went swimming in the ponds at Hampstead. You used to make us get in with you and it was bloody freezing.'

'I didn't make you and besides, you liked it.'

'Ben made me, he said we couldn't let you swim on your own. I remember, he said, you had to do that too often when you were a kid, and it would be good to let you know that you had us now.'

Francis smiled, 'and now we don't.'

Joy nodded. 'And now we don't,' she echoed.

Over the next few months Francis buried himself in parenting, working and swimming. He and the students had sectioned off a part of the college garden and built five raised beds.

'Potatoes in one, courgettes, sweetcorn and broad beans all grow together in two others. We will have onions, cauliflowers, broccoli…We will give it to the food bank, local produce.'

The focus helped, he lost himself in the world and the students stayed late, came at weekends, relished what they were doing, together.

Being at home was harder though. Sometimes, if he was too quiet Rae would sit beside him, put her head on his chest and tell him what songs she was trying to play on her keyboard or something she had learnt at school.

'Soon you will need a proper piano,' he would say.

She would smile and say 'maybe, or maybe I will want to learn a different instrument.'

Later, when Rae was in bed, Victoria said, 'it's like you have a dark cloud following you around,' and he felt guilty, as if he had put it there on purpose.

And then his mother called.

'Francis, the cancer is back son, the doctor says it is in me, deep in me. I'm sorry son.'

He decided to walk to the beach, walk the way he used to run when he was little. It had been a long time since he had been there, a long time since he had swum there. He walked quickly away from the house, he had always moved as fast as he could when he left there.

It was mid-tide and he had forgotten which way the current would be moving, but he didn't really care. He undressed quickly, piled his things together up against the old slipway, and got into the water. He didn't swim far out, he wanted to feel safe so instead he swam along the line of the promenade, feeling the flat grey water lap against him, watching the bow wave form around him as he breathed. He stopped for a while, faced outward. It was flat and empty. He thought he might cry but he didn't.

The sea tells you how you feel, he thought. 'Numb,' he said out loud as he stood up in the shallows, 'afraid.' And as he left the water and walked toward his clothes, he added, 'guilty.'

'Warm water for this time of year, don't you think?' came a voice from the promenade above him as he was pulling his trousers on.

Francis turned slowly, gathering the energy required to be polite to a stranger, but it wasn't a stranger. The swimmer had greyer hair and his face had more and deeper lines, but he was unmistakable. Still tanned, stocky, and wearing what could have been exactly the same faded blue track suit bottoms he had worn thirty years earlier.

'I don't think I have seen you here…before?'

'I've not swum here for a very long time, over thirty years.'

The swimmer wandered down the slipway staring at him intently. As he drew closer he smiled and said, 'Francis?'

'Hello,' said Francis, sounding like a child again.

'It's been a long time,' the swimmer said. 'You look well. How's life?'

'It's in progress, I have a family, a daughter, I swim. How are you?'

'I swim too.' The swimmer said laughing.

And then they stopped talking and just stared at each other. Francis felt a prickle behind his eyes and he looked toward the water and away from the northerly wind.

'How is your mother?'

'She is dying.'

'I'm sorry.'

'She had more time than she might have, eh?' Francis said quietly. And then, 'was it real?'

'Was what real?'

'The contract.'

'What do you think?'

'I live as though it is real.'

'So, it is real.'

'And if I wanted another…' Francis wasn't sure where those words had come from. He had always imagined that if he saw the swimmer again he would just say thank you but that was not what came out of his mouth. He reddened, again feeling like a child.

'Another what?'

'Exchange.'

'How old is your mother, Francis?'

'Old.'

'How old will be old enough do you think?'

'It is a strange idea,' Francis whispered.

'What is?'

'Choosing not to save your mother's life?' He felt tears begin to rise 'You see, I become a child again the moment I see you.' He clasped both hands to his head as if trying to hold himself together. He was crying properly now. 'It's about letting go, right?'

'What is?'

'Seeing you? Now? I'm letting go or something.'

'Are you?'

'Yes. No. Yes.'

'I don't know son, I'm not sure seeing me has to mean anything and I don't really know what letting go actually means.'

'I have a good life. I have a daughter now as well; did I tell you? Her name is Rae, she is so…so wonderful. I tell you, when she opens her eyes wide I think the whole world is going to fall into them and be better for it.'

'That's lovely to hear Francis, I am so pleased for you.'

'I've never forgotten you.'

'Nor I you,' the swimmer said.

'Rae will be thirty when I am gone, and I sort of hope she will have kids by then and not just one, but two of three or five, because it will be easier to not have me if she has her own children, you know?'

'Perhaps,'

'And when I was out there swimming I was thinking of my friend Ben. You would have loved Ben, but he died and I miss him and I think about him when I swim, he was very good with wood, you know.' Francis was wiping his eyes with his hands and his towel. 'He used to say that he wanted to be a better man, that he wanted to be good, noble.'

'Sounds like a good thing to want; we all want to be better

than we are, don't we?'

'Do we? Ben was only forty-four when he died.'

'That's no age is it.'

'When he told me he was ill, I thought maybe that I should come here, look for you, see...see if perhaps I could help him?'

The swimmer said nothing, he stared at the sea, not moving, barely acknowledging that Francis was talking.

'I told him...I told him about you and about our contract.'

'Do you think he believed you?'

'I don't know.'

'Would you believe someone if they told you that?'

'He told me off,' Francis ignored the question. 'I said that if I could help him I would, if I could find you and make an exchange for him I would.'

'That was rash young Francis.'

Francis laughed as he cried, 'that was pretty much what he said.'

'Sounds like a wise young man.'

'I think my mother sent me to the beach so that she could die in peace,'

'Like she used to send you here so she could make your tea?'

'She didn't send me here. I just came.'

'If you say so.'

'How many years would it take to save my mum?' Francis was not looking at the swimmer now; he was following the old man's gaze out across the slate grey sea.

The swimmer stayed silent.

'Now,' said Francis, 'to make the cancer go away again, how many years?'

'I've nothing for you, son. I'm sorry but there is no deal to be made today.'

'Why not?'

'I just haven't.'

'But why?'

'Look son, I told you that the cancer would not come back for thirty years and it didn't. I am sorry you lost your friend, and I am sorry your mother is ill but there is nothing you can do, there is nothing for you here.'

'But I just need one more gift from you. That's what it felt like to me. It felt like a gift that you gave me, you know? A gift for my mum.'

'Yes,' said the swimmer, 'and so should this.'

'What, not being able to help my dying mother is a gift?'

'No son, staying beside your daughter for as long as possible is the gift. And not being given the responsibility to choose who to give your life away for, your mother or your daughter. That is the gift.'

'That's what Ben said.'

'Like I said, wise man.'

Francis slumped to the floor, let his head slip down between his knees and he cried. He didn't know how long for but it felt like a long time. He cried for Ben and he cried for Rose. He sat, face down, listening to the sound of the waves and watched the tears drip from his face on to the concrete promenade. When he finally lifted his head up and wiped his eyes the swimmer had gone.

When Francis got back to the house, he walked round to the back door, opened and closed it quietly and walked through the kitchen in to the living room. As soon as he saw her, he knew she was dead. Her right arm was hanging from the side of the chair and it made her body look untidy in a way she would never have allowed if she had life left in her.

He picked it up, rested it across her lap, and stroked her hand.

'Thirty extra years,' he said quietly as he knelt on the floor in front of her, 'and you got to meet your granddaughter. That's all right, isn't it, Mum?'

Gift Three

16

Francis was forty-four when he buried his mother. It was raining outside and there were less than twenty people in the church. Water was dripping down onto the tiled floor from where one of the windows leaked and if Rose had been there he would have teased her by asking why God didn't just fix it, but she wasn't so he just smiled to himself and then felt embarrassed when he saw the vicar staring at him.

'It was a small life,' Francis said to Victoria.

'You say that like it is a bad thing,' she said, 'and it isn't.'

Aunt Ruby was there, although she didn't know it. Her dementia prevented her from recognising her own children, let alone Francis. He felt that when she saw him, her instinct kicked in and she hissed quietly like an old, unhappy cat. Rae stayed close to Francis, holding his finger tightly, leaning into him.

'Who is that lady?' Rae asked.

'She is Nanny's sister; she has had dementia for quite a long time. She doesn't remember Nanny at all, she is probably quite confused being here.'

'That is sad,' said Rae.

'Yes,' said Francis without feeling.

After the service the mourners went to the back room of the same tired old pub that had hosted Rose and Percy's wedding reception and they ate sandwiches and crisps out of bowls. Most of the people there were old friends of Rose's even though they had not seen her for years. They sat in chairs lined up against the wall, struggling to recognise each other.

'It's not really a wake,' Francis whispered to Victoria. 'It's more of a queue isn't it?'

Joy was there too, sitting next to Victoria.

'Thank you,' Francis had whispered to her after the service.

'Of course,' she said.

'You only met her once.'

'I liked her. And anyway, I'm here for you.' She kissed him on the cheek, adding, 'and Rae.'

When they got home Francis sat on the floor beside Rae as she lay in bed.

'I miss Nanny,'

'Me too,' Francis said, stroking her head, 'she loved you very much.'

'What do you think happens when people die?' She asked.

'Well, Nanny believed that if you lived well you went to heaven.'

'If there is a heaven,' Rae said quietly, 'and people think it is a good place, why don't they all just want to go there now?'

'Maybe deep down we know life is best?'

'Nanny was old wasn't she.'

'She was darling.'

'You're not, are you daddy.'

'Me? Nooo, I'm very young.'

Rae closed her eyes and Francis stayed there stroking her head until she was asleep.

When he went downstairs, Victoria was sitting in the living room, the television was off and she had made them both tea.

'Rae doesn't want us to die,' he said to her.

'I'm with her on that.'

He sat down beside Victoria

'Hard day? How are you?' she said.

'Do you think I let her down?'

'Rose?'

'Yes.'

'No and neither did she.'

'I have always felt, I don't know, maybe everyone feels this, but that I was a disappointment somehow…'

'I think most people who think, think that at some point, but it's not a real thought is it? It is a feeling. You were no disappointment. When she was here last, she was asking about your job. I told her about the students growing vegetables and giving them to people. She didn't know you did that.'

'I didn't think she would be interested.'

'She was, she was proud.' That night he dreamt he was in the middle of an ocean. It was completely flat and unfathomably deep. He could not see land, did not know which way to swim and began to feel heavy. His breathing began to accelerate, and he woke with a start. Victoria was beside him, stroking his arm, shushing him, telling him it was ok. He said he was sorry and laid awake trying to picture his mother's idea of heaven. Even there, he thought, with all the people she expected to see, she would be lonely.

Three days after the funeral Francis drove back to

Birchington to empty his mother's house. The council had acknowledged her passing and told him that he had two weeks to return the keys to them so they could pass them to the next tenant. Part of him wanted to object; to ask for more time so he could go through his mother's things, pass them on to her neighbours, think about them, remember her, but in truth there were very few things. Rose had a jewellery box with fake pearls and cheap rings in, that would be for Rae. There was a fridge, an oven and a washing machine that he had bought her. They would go to neighbours or the Salvation Army. There were clothes that would go to a charity shop. It felt important to him to give things that were useful to people who might need them, *Rose would have liked that* he thought, but after a few hours he found himself mostly just wanting to leave, to get out of the house, and he wondered if his mother had sensed that every time he was there.

There was a cupboard in what had been his bedroom. It had a chest of drawers pushed up against it and Francis could not remember the last time it had been opened. He pushed the draws away and opened it up. It smelt musky and contained a few old board games and two cardboard boxes. One was full of old blankets, he vaguely remembered them from when he was young, there was mould growing on them. The other was piled with the sort of things that Rose did not use but could not bear to throw out. There were pictures he had drawn at school as a child and some roller skates someone had given him but were already broken. And there was a box, the box in which Francis had kept the letters he had written to Patricia.

He hesitated before he opened it, embarrassed at the memory, but he opened it anyway and began to read the scrawled handwriting of a kid who had invented an American pen pal secure in the knowledge that a real person would not want to write to him, or perhaps he could not tell a real person the truth.

My dad died last week. I didn't go to the funeral, my mum says that funerals are not for children. I keep expecting him to come back through the door and I would have to pretend to be pleased. When he used to leave he usually came back and it felt like a trick. Sometimes I wonder if this is a trick.

He had no recollection of having written that, let alone thought it or felt it. He sat down on the floor, leaned against the bed and read every letter. He liked the first one best,

Hello, my name is Francis, I live in a small village in Kent, I don't have many friends, I like running. I would like to know more about the world, maybe you will tell me?

It felt as though the letters didn't belong to him, but to some other little boy and he resolved to burn them, but not quite yet, and not there. He would take them home, read them again, burn them later.

By the end of the day all that was left was a small house with worn out carpets and no Rose. Francis phoned the first house clearance man he could find and paid him to empty the house of everything. While the man did that Francis drove to a garden centre, bought a miniature apple tree and a plum tree, one for Rose and one for Rae. He planted them in the corner of the back garden, then he left, and did not look back as he drove away.

*   *   *

'I really want to learn to play the guitar,' Rae announced over breakfast one Saturday five months later.

'Are you bored with the piano?'

'No but it isn't very mobile, is it?'

'That really little one Joy bought you is…'

'Daaad,' she raised her eyebrows.

'Do you want to be able to play music with other people?' Victoria asked.

'No.'

'Heaven forbid,' Francis said sarcastically, and Rae raised her eyebrows again announcing to her parents that she did not feel she was being taken seriously.

'Maybe Auntie Joy could help?'

'Cool,' said Rae.

Maybe a guitar will help her mix a bit more,' Victoria said to Francis after Rae had gone to school, 'she is quite a…a self-contained little girl.'

'She is a bit of a loner.'

'She is, but let's face it, given her parents we can't be surprised, can we?'

The thought, *a sibling would have helped,* crossed Francis's mind but he said nothing. Victoria saw it anyway.

'I would have loved another child too, you know.' Looking away, gathering plates together loudly.

'I know,' Francis said. He put his arm round her and kissed on the cheek, 'I honestly do know.'

Victoria turned into him and rested her head on his chest. 'I'm sorry,' she said.

'Hey,' he kissed her again. 'It's all right, it is done; you were right.' He stepped back, put his arms on her shoulders and looked at her. 'You were right, I should have done more to make sure you knew that. It would have been risky, we might have lost our balance and fallen over, and who wants to fall over?'

Later that day Francis phoned Joy. She still lived in Hackney in the large one-bedroom basement flat she had bought with the money she surprised herself earning playing guitar and keyboards for a band that was, for three years in the 1990s, quite big in Japan. She was the most energetic person Francis had ever known. Always busy, always engaged, always going or coming back from somewhere interesting or ridiculous: Libya, Vietnam, South Korea, El Salvador, Mexico, all in the last year; yet she had been the first person to phone Francis when his mother died, and she came to the funeral, postponing a trip to America in order to be there.

'How are you?' she asked as soon as he said hello.

He went to say, *ok*, but it felt crass. Joy deserved more.

'I'm quiet,' he said. 'I think I am still rearranging my internal furniture, and I don't think I had finished doing that from Ben...'

'It will take a little while, you and your mum...well it's not like moving the odd desk and chair, is it? You are going to have to take the carpets up, Francis.'

'Yes, it will take a while. How are you?'

'I'm good, I think. I saw Carlos last week. He had been on a date, and I think he felt he needed to tell me, to sort of confess. I told him that it's what Ben would have wanted, although it feels odd to be cast in the role of...I don't know...some sort of emotional policewoman...you know? I do wonder what it will be like if I stop working so much, I feel like I am avoiding something but...I don't know...I like being busy.'

'Where next?'

'Berlin, two weeks, why?'

'Because my daughter wants to learn guitar and...'

'Oh how exciting, does she have a guitar?'

'No not yet...I thought you might tell me what to buy, to start her off with?'

'She could use the one Ben made me.'

'Whoa, I don't know if something like that is right for a beginner.'

'Oh of course it is, they should be played, and Ben would have loved that. And I love that. Can you come up here? I can get her started.'

Rae and Francis visited the following weekend. Joy had a large, sprawling, yellow-walled living room that she used as a studio. It had guitars, keyboards, amplifiers and recording equipment as well as a tapestry loom.

'What is that for?' Rae asked. 'It looks like a harp made of wool.'

'A new hobby, in case I need quiet.'

Joy and Rae sat down in the middle of the room on two stools, the guitar Ben had made was on a stand next to them.

'What do you think of when you think of Ben?' Joy asked as if she were talking to a grown up.

'I remember the way he made me feel. I think everyone must remember that about Uncle Ben.'

'Out of the mouths of babes,' said Joy. 'He made this guitar, he would have liked the idea of you playing it.'

Francis sat in the corner while Joy patiently showed Rae four chords. He watched his daughter lean into the body, curving her back like a bow, her small hands shaking with the tension of holding down the steel strings. When she lifted her hand, the tips of her fingers had dents in them and she smiled with pride. Watching her made his insides feel lighter, as if a friendly sea was lifting him up, propelling him forward just a little.

Brighter than you, Rose had said, and he knew what she had meant. It wasn't as simple as her being a child who loved life and he an adult who was grieving its losses. It was more that the world thrilled her, and that thrill demanded she give it all of her rapt attention. When he was young, he was afraid. He'd had to work hard to make that go away but it never felt completely banished. Rae was close to fearless; it was born of knowing she was safe. *She will grow out of this innocence,* he told himself, *when she discovers cynicism, boys, failure, disappointment or cruelty.* That was what growing up was or threatened to be, a sullying of wonder. He would watch for when that happens, he will be sad when it comes, but for now he would revel in its absence, celebrate the way she seized new things, maybe even try to learn from it.

'We should perhaps stop now?' Joy said gently, putting her guitar down.

'Why?' asked Rae, holding on to hers like it was a friend.

'Partly because you don't want to hurt your fingers so much that you won't be able to practice tomorrow, but mostly because your dad is crying.'

Within eighteen months, Rae had learnt to play all of the songs Joy gave her to learn and a few others she had chosen herself and had relished turning inside out. She was at secondary school now and she said she liked the way things were divided up into different subjects. She particularly enjoyed Art, Biology and English, but it was her first tentative steps in music classes that she seemed to enjoy the most. She had been learning piano for three years, had taken exams and was received appreciatively by the school music teacher for playing stiffly but adequately. She spent lunch times practicing in the music room and this made Francis and

Victoria worry that she was spending too much time on her own.

'Do you not want to spend time with your friends?' Francis had asked nervously.

'Well, no,' Rae said. 'Obviously not.'

When Christmas came the kids were told to put on some sort of show and asked if any of them had anything they would like to do. Rae, volunteered to sing a song

'Don't be nervous sweetie,' Victoria said nervously.

'I'm not,' Rae replied, 'it's just a song.'

On the evening of the performance, when her turn came, Rae shyly, tentatively and very carefully carried the guitar Ben had made for Joy on to the stage. She took a moment to pull the strap over her shoulder and then played a lilting, gentle song called *You Missed My Heart,* sung from the perspective of a vengeful murderer. She played it as though nobody else was there, looking sometimes at her fingers on the fretboard and sometimes at the floor. Francis noticed, through misted eyes, that she didn't acknowledge the clapping when it came, but she did stroke the guitar.

'She did good,' Francis said to Victoria with relief.

'She really did, and people liked her,'

When Rae had come and found them after the concert they applauded and she shrugged.

'Was it fun? Did you enjoy it?'

'It was ok,' she shrugged again, 'I wouldn't want to do it all the time though.'

'Because of the audience?' Francis asked.

'Maybe' she said, 'I think music is…I don't know, I don't think it needs to have anything to do with other people. I like playing it on my own the best.'

'On the one hand,' Francis would say to Victoria that night, 'we know her better than we have ever known anyone, but on the other we have no idea who she will be.'

'She could have been a poet or she could have been a fool,' sang Victoria, before adding, 'Do you want something by *Queen* next?'

'She doesn't go to parties.'

'Neither did I.'

'Or socialise much?'

'Did you?'

'No, that's why I worry, I don't want her to have a childhood like mine.'

Victoria sighed, 'well she hasn't, for one thing she has two parents.'

✳   ✳   ✳

Over time new routines evolved. Victoria worked hard and slept deep. Rae went to school, read, played guitar, and more reluctantly piano, and got taller. Francis would get up very early in the morning, whenever light was breaking, and, still imagining that being in the sea slowed down time, cycle to the beach whilst the girls were asleep. On some days, with a north wind and cloudless sky, it was bitingly cold and close to silent. He would try to swim outward until he noticed his body telling him to turn around, the fear that had infected him since he had dragged the unconscious woman from the storm, rising up uninvited in him. When the fear subsided he would turn parallel with the beach, and swim into the current. He would be home in time to make a cup of tea for Victoria before she woke and breakfast for Rae before she went to school. Rae was always quiet in the mornings and Francis instinctively fussed around her. He worried that school made her unhappy, he worried that she always walked there on her own and came back alone too, that she didn't arrange to do things with other children at the weekends, and that she rarely spoke about friends. He worried that she was like him.

'I'm ok Dad,' she would say, raising her eyebrows. 'I have exactly what I need and I don't want more. If I did, I would do something about it.'

'When do you laugh?' he would ask.

'When you cook.'

And when the three of them were together they did laugh, as they had always done. Victoria was principal of her college now and she had started wearing two piece suits and sensible shoes

'You look like a lawyer,' Francis would say.

'If I were a lawyer you would be in prison.'

'What for, I'm innocent,'

'You'd be in prison for being annoying.'

'You would dad,' Rae would join in, 'you are annoying.'

'It's a fair cop, but I had accomplices, if I give them up – it's you two by the way – can I cut a deal?'

Since Rae had been born Francis had planted forty-seven fruit trees, nine of them in London, one in Thanet at the end of his mother's garden and the rest around Brighton. He kept a list in a small notebook; what and where they were and when he had planted them. He cycled past one of them every time he went to the beach. He had the vaguest sense that if he saw it every day he would not notice it growing and that time would slow down. But it grew, and it bore fruit and he got older.

He was forty eight now, *two thirds of the way through,* but he wasn't as desperate as he had been, nor as afraid of time passing. *I have already had longer than Ben,* he reasoned, *and I am not alone.*

Occasionally, Victoria and Francis made love. Afterwards, sometimes, they lay together and one of them would say to the other, 'So, how are you, really?'

'Good, I think.'

'You?'

'I'm good. Thank you for asking.'

Sometimes they reflected on what Francis referred to as middle-aged sex

'Did you leave your socks on?'

'My feet are cold and it's not like we're courting.'

'Courting,' laughed Francis, 'what a great word.'

Other times Victoria would refer to sex as 'a reminder I am in the world and in my body,' which scared Francis enough to ask her where she was the rest of the time. 'Working,' she said, and went to sleep.

They were all happy, comfortable and bound together. Francis visited his uncertainties in the sea, reminded of frailties he didn't have elsewhere and he was grateful for that. It seemed ironic to him that the sea, the place he had always escaped to had become the place he went to be afraid now but some part of him considered it another exchange with the universe, *you are a lucky man, don't take that for granted,* and by the time he was dry he was as settled as he could expect to be.

It may have carried on like that for years; sometimes things do. Those last seventeen years of his life might have rushed by and before he knew it he would be approaching sixty-five and wrapping up his affairs. Telling Rae, that he loved her, as he had done every day, and that whatever it was she was doing and whoever it was she did it with, not to forget to continue to do the things she loved. Perhaps also there would be a note to Victoria thanking her for being his friend, his partner, and trying as hard as possible to not say sorry to her for something he didn't quite understand but felt anyway. But it didn't carry on like that. Sometimes things don't.

17

His name was Kevin Pierce. Not that Francis or Victoria cared. The people closest to him said that he had depression and mental health. Victoria said that she hated people who said things like that, nearly as much as she hated the man who had killed six people, injured thirteen others, and left her daughter in a coma.

'Had mental health. What the fuck does that mean? He quite clearly didn't have any fucking mental health at all did he? The hateful bastard.'

Francis would have hated too if only he could have breathed.

Pierce had lost his job with the building firm he worked for. He was always late, sometimes not showing up at all. Once, at a job in Portslade he turned up drunk and said loudly to the woman who's house they were working on, 'you don't wear makeup much do you? You should love, you'd look alright if you made a bit of an effort. Can I pop the kettle on eh?' He was sent home and even though he apologised the next day his boss, a man called Lee, who believed good manners were the cornerstone of a successful business, decided he didn't need an unreliable obnoxious bloke, who wasn't even a good plumber, working for him.

'There were plenty of other people who would love your job.'

'Oh, I'm disposable, am I?' Pierce had said.

'Well, yeah,' said Lee. 'Obviously. So, fuck off.'

Three years earlier Pierce had been engaged to be married to Kirsty, but she broke it off after she found out he had been sending suggestive texts to her younger cousin. After he was sacked he hit the bottle harder and began to bombard Kirsty with messages, telling her that he had made a mistake, that he had matured, that they were meant to be together and that he wanted to marry her. Seeing Kirsty had not heard from him since throwing a white wine spritzer in his face in the Three Crowns two and a half years earlier, she was very surprised to hear from him. This surprise was compounded by the fact that she had married a man called Gavin a year earlier and was six months pregnant.

Kevin was very angry when Gavin told him to leave his wife alone. An anger that was made all the more acute it seems by the fact that Gavin was black. Words were exchanged, threats made. Police reports later confirmed that Kirsty had reported dog excrement being put through the couple's letterbox, and Kevin had been photographed by Kirsty as he followed her to and from work. The police did speak to Kevin, who was outraged at the suggestion that his wife-to-be did not want him near her and astonished to hear that she imagined that any dog excrement put through her letterbox, not that he knew anything about that, could possibly have anything to do with her, it would surely have been aimed at Gavin, Kevin claimed.

'The nurse?' the Police asked.

'Yeah him', Kevin spat, 'what sort of man is a nurse anyway?'

A restraining order meant that Kevin couldn't be within five hundred metres of Kirsty, so standing outside her house without a policeman being called was very hard. However, none of this made Kevin less angry; in fact, his rage spiralled outward. It now included the police and of course it included Gavin and all the male nurses and black people and pregnant people and as the fire in him spread he realised he had to let it out. He was a man of action, he would say it out loud to himself after a few drinks, 'And it's time to do some action.'

None of this had anything to do with Rae. She was doing something that Francis was disproportionately excited about: meeting a friend from school in a coffee shop on a Saturday morning . He had made a fuss, as if it were a date or a job interview.

'It's no big deal,' Rae had smiled, 'she is interested in learning guitar and we get on. People do it all the time, Dad.'

'Yeah, people do,' Francis said. 'But you don't.'

Rae liked the fuss he was making. She liked that he noticed when she did new things, particularly when they were things that she might, possibly, secretly, consider quite scary. Whenever Francis encouraged her to come for a swim with him in the sea, she had made excuses, finally admitting she thought it was scary.

'It is unsettling,' Francis agreed, 'but that doesn't mean it is dangerous.'

'I think it is murky, you can't see what is beneath you. There are too many variables,'

My little girl just used the word variables, thought Francis and he smiled, because of course she was right.

Rae was learning a song called *Low Expectations* by Edwyn

Collins. It required what she called a hammer pinkie, where she had to put her little finger on and off the string really quickly. She couldn't get it right. She was sitting at a table at the side of Roxie's Cafe waiting for her friend, tapping her little finger on the table.

'She's always had a thing for corners.' Victoria said.

'Thank Christ for that,' Francis replied.

Kevin Pierce knew that Gavin would stop by Roxie's Café for coffees on Saturday morning. He had watched him leave the flat he shared with Kirsty, stop at the newsagents and the bakers and then go to the café for takeaway coffees, which he would no doubt take back to Kirsty, climb into bed and be in the space that Kevin should be in. The utter bastard.

Kevin's old white van had failed its MOT, and in his rage he had considered crashing it into the garage that carried out the inspection but that would be a waste. People might think that was an accident, a brake problem that had actually come up in the MOT and anyway it would not address the issue of Gavin. If he was going to weaponise his eighteen-year-old transit van Roxie's Cafe was better. It would make a mess, it would be a statement, it would show the world he was not disposable and it would show Kirsty that he was willing to fight for her, not with frothy coffee and cream cheese bagels but with his heart and his soul and a van that didn't have legal brake pads.

Roxie's Cafe was on the corner of West and Stack Road. There was a pedestrian crossing about forty metres before you reached the cafe, and as Pierce approached, with four small cans of petrol in the back of the van – which he imagined would ignite on impact for no reason other than that was what seemed to happen on television when cars with petrol in them hit buildings – the lights turned red. Kevin was annoyed that he'd had to stop at the lights to let bloody people cross the road but as he drove past Roxie's, to go round the roundabout, he saw Gavin inside. The timing was perfect and the gods were on his side so he did a three-point turn and tried again.

There were people sitting outside the café, a woman was smoking and laughing with a man who was nodding and smiling. He hated them immediately. They were near the door, which would be the weakest part of the building, so Kevin aimed for them. In his mind's eye, which was slightly blurred by the four cans of Stella and two spliffs he had consumed over the preceding hour, he imagined that Gavin, the bloody male nurse, would be on his way out now, walking toward the door and so Kevin closed his eyes, put his foot down to the floor of his unresponsive and heavy van and ploughed through the bodies and the first five tables and the people sitting at them and into the wooden cabinet that had the leaflets and the water on.

Kevin Pierce braced himself for the explosion. He thrust his arm through the open window of the van in what was intended as an announcement that he had arrived at this point on purpose and was neither disposable nor unlovable. It looked to one shocked bystander as though the man driving the van was waving and perhaps trying to say sorry. Kevin shouted something. Someone said it was a political slogan, others that it was simply, 'Fucking, fucking fuckers.' But the owner of the café, who was at the far end of her coffee shop standing quite still, watching the white van career through the shop she loved, maintained it was just an inarticulate scream with some gargled sobbing attached.

Kevin Pierce did not die. He broke an arm and both legs.

He was crying when the policeman got to him and said dramatically, 'It's going to blow,' and when they opened the back of the van they found four tins of petrol, a U bend pipe, a bathroom sink and a scrawled note claiming that Kirsty had been taken from him against her will by a man using Voodoo. Gavin was in the toilet when the van hit, he was unhurt, the paramedics later commented that the nurse attending to some of the injured while waiting for the ambulances to arrive probably saved lives.

Francis had been swimming and had just got out of the water. He had dried himself, poured himself some tea, and decided to check his phone. There were three voicemails, He had only been in the water for forty minutes. One was from Victoria saying 'Accident. Rae. Phone Me.' The next was from a policewoman, speaking too slowly: 'an incident,' she said. 'Your daughter has sustained injuries.' The next was from Victoria: 'Francis, we have to go to the hospital.' He was dressed within thirty seconds and ran up the shelved beach phoning Victoria as he did.

'What's happening?'

'Someone drove a van into the coffee shop. People are dead. She is hurt, I think it is serious. I've just arrived at the hospital. I have to find her. I'll call you back.' Victoria hung up.

Francis did not know how he drove to the hospital. He could not remember the route he took or if he drove safely. He remembers not knowing where to park and not having money for the parking machine. He used the app on his phone. It asked him how long he wanted, and his chest began to tighten. *All of the hours,* he thought, because he wasn't planning to leave without Rae.

He ran up the hill toward the hospital, texting Victoria:

'Where are you?'

'She is in surgery. I'm on a seat outside the main entrance.'

He found her sitting on a bench, staring at the ground. She looked like a woman who had been boned from the neck down.

'Tell me…' is all he could say, and she glanced up and said what she knew he needed to hear first.

'Alive. Just. She was crushed. It hurt her head, and her chest. I heard them say her pelvis was broken. I think it is her head they are most worried about. Alive.'

Speaking the words had made her dizzy. Francis sat down beside her, he was shaking. He bent close enough to just be touching, shoulder to shoulder. He was bloodless and the air that he was breathing felt like broken glass in his lungs. Victoria stared at the floor.

'Is her friend ok?'

'Yes, she saw it, hadn't arrived. Rae was early. Her parents called me. Said they were praying for Rae, said how much Hannah liked her.'

'Was it an accident?'

'No,' she paused. 'An angry man drove his van into the shop. Killed at least five people. They were just sitting there. Like Rae.'

And then Victoria began to cry. Her shoulders shook first and then her whole body joined in, her grey face lifted enough for Francis to see that whatever she was feeling was going to split her skin and burst out of her, so he turned to her and put his arms round her and held her.

'We have to be there when she comes out of surgery,' he whispered.

'What if she doesn't wake up?'

He didn't say anything, he rested his forehead on hers and breathed deeply.

'Come on,' she said. 'Let's go inside.'

They waited for five hours. Staring at an empty bed in the Intensive Care Unit that had been set aside for Rae on her return from surgery. Francis thought, *she has a bed, they must know she will come round, that she is going to be ok.* Then he imagined someone else being put in the bed and being told that a doctor would be along to talk to them soon. But that didn't happen. Nothing happened at all. They just sat on either side of an empty bed and waited for their daughter.

When the Ward Sister suggested that they might want to get coffee they both said no.

'She will be in post op after the surgery,' the Sister said, 'they will tell me when that happens and I will tell you, ok? I will send someone down so you will be here when she gets back. I promise.'

They went to the café and sat opposite each other holding hands. There were too many hospital emotions swirling around them; relieved spouses, happy grandparents, grieving sons. Francis could feel them all buzzing around in the air. Victoria barely noticed that there were other people on the planet, let alone that they might be feeling anything. She stared at the plastic table until she could bear it no more.

'I want to go back now,' she said, and so they went back.

'I was just going to send someone for you,' they were greeted by the Ward Sister upon their return, 'they have finished the surgery. As far as we can tell, it went well but they are keeping her in an induced coma. There was some swelling round the brain and whilst the surgery has eased that, it needs to be monitored over the next forty-eight hours.'

'Right, but it went well,' Francis said desperately.

'That is what they said. The surgeon will come and talk to you as soon as he can.'

There were two porters and two nurses with Rae when they wheeled her on to the ICU nearly an hour and a half later. Her bed was high and surrounded by two drips, two monitors and as soon as she was in place, two more nurses. Rae's head was heavily bandaged, there was a smear of dried blood on her right cheek, and Francis instinctively wanted to wipe it off but didn't move. Her left arm was bandaged and there was a cage under the covers holding them away from her legs.

When Victoria saw her, she gasped and closed her eyes.

Francis stared at the dried blood on his daughters face and gripped the arms of the wooden chair he was sitting on until his hands hurt. He wanted to touch her head, to stroke her the way he had when she couldn't fall asleep when she was a baby, but he was scared of breaking this fragile little thing, so instead he reached out and touched the end of the bed, because he was near, because he could not begin to imagine that there was life beyond the space his family were in now and because he had no power to do anything else.

18

Francis and Victoria stayed beside Rae for three days. They would take it in turns to go home once a day for a shower and to change their clothes, ensuring one of them was always by Rae's side.

The surgeon who had operated on Rae was a tall, softly spoken man in his late fifties called Mr. Cameron. He had come to Rae's bedside that first night and explained the procedure he had undertaken and that they needed to wait, for now, and let her body heal.

'She has a traumatic brain injury,' he had said, 'and we need to keep her in a coma until the swelling goes down. I don't think the right side of her brain has been damaged, that is important because if she survives...'

'If,' said Victoria.

'I need to be able to tell you the truth.'

'Yes,' Victoria said, 'and I need to stop you sometimes to make sure I hear it.'

'If she survives, and I think it is fifty-fifty, then it is

important that the right-hand side of her brain has not been damaged so that her language and logic skills will remain unaffected. There is a lesion on the left side of her brain. Her retina had been detached and the cornea may be damaged in her right eye. I think she may have some paralysis or at least weakness down her left side, but we can't assess that yet. The priority is for the swelling to reduce so we can fully close her skull. This will take a little time.'

Francis sat staring at the man who was calmly describing his daughter's injuries and then looked at Rae: incubated, comatose, broken. Finally he managed to say, 'thank you.'

Mr. Cameron came every day. In silence he would check the wound on Rae's head, the numbers on the machine and the chart at the end of her bed. After he had done his checks he would make something akin to small talk, and say things like 'she has done well to get this far,' and 'she has long fingers, does she play piano?'

'Yes, and the guitar.' Francis said, and he wondered if he would ever get to hear her finished her rendition of *Low Expectations*, with her hammer pinkie played to perfection.

Five days after the surgery Mr Cameron completed his usual checks and then went outside and returned with a chair. He sat down at the end of Rae's bed, and said to Francis and Victoria, 'I wonder, would you mind telling me a little bit about her? Who she is? What she likes? I like to know the people I work with, and Rae is not able to tell me herself.'

Victoria and Francis told him she was sarcastic, watchful, that she laughed at herself more than others. That she was good at school and shy and self-critical and funny. That she was meeting a friend and that she didn't usually do that sort of thing, and that they had wanted her to go out more and be social and how wrong they were, how they now wished she had stayed in. That she was an only child who played guitar quietly so nobody could hear her, even though she was quite good. That she was only fifteen. They held hands as they did this. Francis realised that this very busy doctor, who probably worked seventy-five hours a week trying to save lives, was giving him something more generously than anything he could remember.

'How is she doing? Please?' Francis asked.

'Well, she is still with us. I would like her to be doing better by now. She is taking her time. Is that in her nature?'

'Not usually,' Victoria said.

'She can be tentative when she is afraid,' Francis said, biting his dry bottom lip.

'She has been through a significant trauma,' Mr. Cameron said. 'If I were her, I would be afraid too.'

After Mr Cameron left Francis gripped Victoria's hand tighter and said, 'If I could, I would kill the man who did this.'

'I won't let him into my head,' Victoria said. 'I will not give him attention.'

'I would not feel a thing as I did it. I have never hurt another human being in my life, but I would kill him.' After he had said this he realised nothing had changed. Rae did not wake up and he did not feel better. He had simply said some words.

'You're right, of course,' he said to Victoria but she didn't answer.

Over the following days Francis sat quietly, looking at his daughter. Sometimes his breathing became shallow, as if his body had forgotten how to inhale, and he would breathe in deeply, two, three, four times and then steady himself, anxious not to take any air that Rae might need. Flowers had come from Rae's school. Hannah had brought them. Shy, embarrassed, perhaps even guilty that she was not hurt too. She began to cry when she saw her friend, and Francis loved her for that.

'If I'd been early…'

'I'm glad you weren't,' said Victoria.

'The school, we, are doing a cake day. We all bake something, and the money we raise, we thought we…we thought we would like to give it to Rae, to replace her guitar. It was a good one, wasn't it?'

'A friend made it for her, a very close friend' Francis said.

'Would they be able to make her another?'

Francis shook his head.

'We miss her,' Hannah blushed.

Later, Victoria said in the tiniest of voices, 'I'm not going home without her.'

'I know.'

'I'm not.'

'I know. We'll stay, together.'

But Victoria was shrinking with every passing day and Francis was retreating into himself, and even though they knew they were there, they had stopped being there together.

'You should consider going home,' Mr Cameron said. 'Perhaps think about trying to do something normal?'

Francis could not remember what normal was. Normal was a luxury afforded to fortunate people, but he knew that the words the man had said were intended to help him in some way, guide them away from this small room, and he also knew that sitting there would not make Rae better. It was the seventh day. Mr Cameron came every evening. Francis and

Victoria still took it in turns to go home to change and wash, to move around the house trying to ignore the silence. Francis had brought back the wooden Dolphin Ben had carved for Rae. Despair and exhaustion invited superstition and he thought perhaps familiarity would help. It made no sense, and he knew it. They were not trying to draw her from her sleep with the smell of familiar things, instead they were waiting for the swelling to go down and for her to be potentially well enough for the anaesthetic that was keeping her asleep to be reduced.

Sometimes, when he dozed on the edge of sleep Francis found himself thinking of the swimmer. He imagined him in the grey bouncing water, like he had been that first time. He imagined him turning in a long arc and swimming toward him and he remembered the last time he had seen him. 'I've nothing for you, son,' he'd said, 'I'm sorry but there is no deal to be made today. Staying beside your daughter for as long as possible is the gift.' And it was but now Francis would give up everything for Rae, every last day, every last minute.

'I'm going to go to Birchington tomorrow.' Francis said to Victoria later that evening.

She just stared at him. He felt he had perhaps said the most stupid sentence of his life. How did he explain that he was going to a beach to ask someone, someone he had never mentioned, to save his daughter's life?

'Why?'

He wanted to tell her. He wanted to say, *because when I was little, I traded in years of my life to save my mother, and it worked and I want to offer the same person who offered me that contract whatever I can to make Rae better.* But the last time he had told someone that secret, his mother had become ill again. Rae was still alive and he did not want to sabotage what felt like the only, ridiculous, desperate, superstitious, pathetic thing he could possible do to save his daughter?

'It is the only place I know to go to…to pray.'

'That makes no sense'

'I can't stand doing nothing.'

'And going to Birchington is doing something?'

'I think it might help.'

'Help who?'

'Just help,' he said quietly.

'Help you?'

'If you like.'

'But you don't believe…' she said, and he didn't know if she meant in God or that their daughter was going to wake up.

Francis kissed his daughter on the forehead, tucked the Dolphin into the side of her bed, and left the ward. Victoria looked as though she was asleep but Francis knew she was awake with her eyes closed and would not open them to see him leave. As he walked quietly toward the lift, he thought, *if you need somewhere to put your rage, you can give it to me. If she doesn't get better, nothing will matter anyway.*

He stopped for takeaway coffee in the hospital café and as he waited for the young man who had no energy for facial expressions to make it, he watched a couple in the corner, huddled together, holding hands. He wanted to ask if their child was ill too, but if they had said yes he would have had nothing to offer that would help, and if they said no, he would envy them. So, he went outside into the cold, walked quickly to his car and set off for Birchington, reasoning he would be there before the sun came up and that he would wait on the beach until it went down again. He was sure that he would see the swimmer, and he knew that his certainty was a form of madness.

*   *   *

Francis must have driven from Brighton to Birchington over a hundred times but driving the same route now he could not remember what he used to think about on those journeys. It might have been places he would like to see before he died; Niagara Falls perhaps, or a garden in Brooklyn, New York or the Highlands of Scotland or a frozen waterfall in Iceland he had seen on the television once. Or conversations he had had with Victoria or Rae, or what to plant, what to pick, what to prune, when to swim. He would have let the comforting and the mundane wash over him and the journey would be done. Now he could not recognise a world that seemed to be continuing as if nothing had happened. He didn't recognise the traffic, the light or the life of the man he had been a week before. He just drove between the only two points that to him still existed. His daughter in her hospital bed and the strip of sea where his despair would lead him to the swimmer.

It was raining when he arrived and he could feel the wind bouncing off his car. He sat in a parking bay overlooking the sea and stared at the sky as it turned from black to grey to reluctant orange. It was mid-tide and although the sea looked relatively benign through the filter of early morning, as it got lighter he could see quite a chop developing. Even so, he got out of his car, opened the boot, took out the swimming bag that was always there and made his way down onto the beach.

He suddenly felt foolish and there was a part of Francis that just wanted to walk to the shore and stare at the water and not get in. To look for the swimmer and wait for him to come but somehow that felt too passive. Sacrifice was required, he knew that deep in his body.

He stood on the slipway where he used to get undressed, staring out at the gathering swell that was coming in from the east and the chop that greeted it about fifty metres out. These were not his conditions. He could feel the fear rising in him and then he saw him, a long way out, red cap, same stroke as always, slow and steady like the first time he had seen him, and Francis knew what he had to do. He had to get in the freezing water and swim out to him. Waiting for the swimmer to turn and come in was not enough. Waiting was not what he was here to do.

Francis didn't bother wrapping a towel around himself to get changed into his trunks, there was nobody else on the beach. He threw his clothes into his bag, put on his orange silicone hat and goggles and walked quickly into the sea. The water was cold but not as cold as the wind, and he was surprised at how quickly he was waist deep. He dived forward, began to swim outwards and he had only swum maybe thirty yards when he got his first reminder of fear. He swallowed it, with a bit of seawater, and swam on.

After another fifty yards he stopped, out of his depth, and when he tried to look outward the swell was too high for him to see where the swimmer was. He was going to have to guess where he would be and wherever it was it would be a lot further from the beach than this. Francis put his head down and began to swim harder. He started counting the strokes: fifty, sixty, seventy. He could feel something electric in his chest and his breathing was getting quicker even though his stroke wasn't. He wanted to get to one hundred strokes, but the swell had drained him and he stopped to try to steady his breathing. He pulled his goggles up and looked outward into the swell, a wave hit him and the salt water stung his eyes. He told himself not to turn and look at the beach, but he turned around anyway. He couldn't see it, just the pulsating water rising all around him. He was far out, and it occurred to him that if he began to sink he would not know what to do, if swimming failed him he would die here, earlier than he was supposed to, and the pain he felt for Rae would die too, but that would be of no use to her. And Victoria? She would hate him for what could only look to her like cowardice and desertion.

'Bollocks to this,' he said out loud and he began swimming again but his chest refused to hold the air he had inhaled, and he stopped again. He laid on his back, looked up and watched the heavy clouds moving lethargically across sky. There he was in a cold grey sea a hundred miles from his comatose daughter imagining that he was doing something for his child. Imagining that what was happening to her was somehow about him. *There is nothing like the sea to remind you that you are insignificant,* he thought, and then he turned and began to swim again, slowly, southeast, in the vain hope that in that swirling ocean, somehow he would bump into a magical old man.

He was concentrating on counting his strokes, wondering what it would be like to go back to Victoria to say that he had failed. 'How can you fail to pray?' She would ask if she would speak at all. And it was then he caught sight of the red cap and the right elbow of the swimmer, lifting high in the water, maybe twenty metres further out, swimming at the same pace as Francis, at the same pace as always.

Francis put his head down and swam harder, struggling

to keep up with the old man but determined not to lose him. He ploughed on through the swell, the rain now coming down, until he arrived at the slope where he had first seen the swimmer nearly forty years earlier. They trod water for a moment, staring at each other and then the swimmer pointed at the promenade, beckoning Francis to get out with him. They both put their heads down, swam closer to the slope, stopped and the swimmer nodded for Francis to go first. He waited for a wave to come and help, he let it lift him on to the slope and he started running, when he turned to look in the water the swimmer was beside him, jogging awkwardly up the concrete toward his towel which was, as it had been that first time, stashed away behind a beach hut.

'What are you doing here?'

'I was looking for you,' replied Francis breathlessly. He felt naked and cold.

'Where is your towel and your clothes?'

'Don't worry about my clothes, I need your help.'

The swimmer was drying himself now, shaking his head and Francis stared at him, shivering.

'Is that rude, I'm sorry.'

'When did you get here?'

'I drove from Brighton. Through the night, came straight here.'

'Have you eaten anything? Do you have a hot drink?'

Francis shook his head. He was beginning to remember what it was to be twelve.

'I'm sorry,' he said.

'Stop saying sorry. You drove?'

'Yes.'

'So let's go and get you dressed and sit in your car.'

The swimmer threw on his clothes, gave Francis a spare towel to wrap around himself and they walked quickly along the promenade to where Francis had left his things. Francis was shaking now, unable to talk, so he concentrated on getting dressed, turning away from the swimmer to put on his trousers, unable to do up the buttons on his shirt. All the time the swimmer watched, occasionally shaking his head. Within a few minutes they were both sitting in the car, engine on, heaters up to full. The swimmer poured hot tea into the cup from his flask and drank some, looking to see if Francis could hold a cup without spilling it all over himself. He couldn't, so he waited. 'My daughter was in an accident, a terrible one, she is very ill…'

Francis told him everything, in shorter sentences than he wanted to. His breathing was still accelerated, his feet and jaw were numb, his hands still shaking.

'I know this may be madness. Christ, swimming out to you, in this, it is insane but I'm…' he wanted to say lost but that felt vague. 'I'm desperate, I need you to help me. Please. I don't even know if in asking for help, I somehow break something, the rules or a contract or a secret, I don't know…'

'What happened to your mum son?'

'My mum died over four years ago,' he said.

'I'm sorry,'

'On the same day that I last saw you.'

'I got the impression you expected as much, but I am sorry.'

'Don't be, I had over thirty more years with her, thanks to you.'

'It's not me, Francis; well, not just me.'

'I want to give you everything I have left, for my daughter. Please.'

'How old are you?'

'Forty-nine.'

'Sixteen years?'

'Less, I turn fifty in ten months.' Suddenly Francis felt like he wasn't offering enough and he started to cry. 'It is all I have.' He looked at the swimmer who was just staring out at the horizon. 'Is it enough?'

'When someone offers everything they have, it is always enough, son.'

'I swear, I'll get in that sea right now and just keep swimming, if you tell me my girl...'.

'Don't be so dramatic,' the swimmer chided. He sat quietly, breathing very deeply. Francis watched him, wiping his eyes and nose on his sleeve, and feeling that it was wise not to talk. The swimmer had closed his eyes and leant in towards Francis.

'You have a few months son. The 7th of November will be your last day.'

'A week before my birthday?'

The swimmer nodded. 'Is it.'

'And Rae? Will she be ok?'

'I need to go now, son,' said the swimmer, and he opened the car door, 'Can I have my towel back?'

Francis handed him the towel as the swimmer got out of the car.

'Good luck son. I'm sorry I couldn't offer you a better deal.'

He closed the car door, turned and walked down toward the promenade and within a minute he was out of sight.

Francis got his phone out and texted Victoria with cold shaking fingers. 'I'm coming back now. How is she?' He waited but there was no reply. He dried his face again, ready to begin the drive, but before reversing out on to the road he saw the swimmer again, stripped down to his trunks and walking back toward the sea. He didn't turn around, he didn't hesitate, he simply waded into the now higher tide and started swimming.

19

Victoria was sitting in the same chair, in the same position when Francis returned to Rae's bedside. She did not lift her head to see him, even though she must have heard him coming into the room. He touched her on the shoulder and asked quietly, 'Any change?' She didn't flinch from the contact nor respond, for all Francis knew she could be sharing her daughter's coma.

'She will be ok, I know you don't believe me, but...' he said, knowing it sounded absurd but believing it had to be said. Then he returned to his seat, reached over to his daughter's hand, and stroked the end of her middle finger.

'What if she had woken up and you weren't here?' said Victoria, staring at Francis with all the rage in the world.

'She's going to be all right, Vic.'

Nurses came in every twenty or thirty minutes, each it seemed charged with a different task. One would check the monitor, two would move Rae slightly to guard against pressure sores, and one came in to check her wound.

'Hmm, that is looking a tiny bit better,' the nurse murmured, barely audible yet enough to lift Victoria back into life.

Francis didn't move, so laced with superstition now that he believed anything he did could somehow undo magic. The nurse turned away from Rae to see both Francis and Victoria staring at her.

'Let's wait and see what the doctor thinks shall we?' An hour later Mr. Cameron came in, with another Doctor who had accompanied him a few times before. Mr. Cameron introduced him anyway.

'This is Dr Shah; I value his opinion.'

Francis nodded and said nothing.

Victoria said, 'the nurse said...'

'Yes, that is why we are here. To have a little look.'

He spent less than a minute looking at Rae's head and then turned away to look at the readings on the monitor. Dr Shah stepped forward and examined Rae as well.

'What do you think?' Mr Cameron asked.

'Looks good, much better' Dr Shah said.

'I think we might try to help her wake up then.'

'Try?' said Victoria.

'Yes, I am not going to take anything for granted, but let us see, shall we?'

After they had gone, Francis said to Victoria, 'It is going to be ok, I think it will be ok.'

'Why, because you went and left us, how does that make anything ok?'

Francis said nothing, he just stared at his daughter.

Twenty minutes later, an anaesthetist and a nurse came in. The anaesthetist went to the monitor that stood beside Rae's bed and spent some time with her back to the room, her attention fully on whatever she was doing, when she finally turned she smiled and said, 'It's Rae, isn't it?' And then, 'it is possible, in some cases, that the patient has been able to hear you. Have you been talking to her?'

'Off and on,' said Francis.

'And each other?'

They didn't answer.

Francis and Victoria were both standing, they had moved to the corner of the room, staring as the nurse organised the sheets around Rae. Francis could not imagine what she was doing, other than simply being present. The anaesthetist pulled back one of Rae's eyelids, then returned to the monitor. Francis just stared at his daughter, whatever the doctor was doing was not having an effect. Rae lay as lifeless as before, asleep, still. When she was a baby he used to like watching her sleep, in part because it meant he might be able to sleep himself but mostly because she looked so safe, so serene. Here now, she looked absent, empty.

But then one of Rae's eyes opened.

'Hello Rae, my name is Dr Vernon, can you hear me?'

Rae's other eye opened slowly and she tried to focus on the Doctor.

'Your mum and dad are here with you Rae.'

Rae turned her gaze to the corner where they were standing, there was a flicker of something, around the mouth, a smile, a twitch?

'Rae, you were in an accident, you have been asleep for a few days and we have been worried about you. Do you understand?'

Rae turned back to the doctor and stared for a few seconds, then she gave a single nod.

Victoria grabbed Francis's arm and squeezed it very tightly.

'Hello baby,' she said. Rae blinked.

'Rae, I am going to go to the foot of the bed, when I ask, could you wiggle your toes for me please?'

Dr Vernon pulled back the sheets, took out a pencil from her breast pocket and ran it along Rae's right foot. Her toes twitched. She did the same on her left foot and they twitched too. 'Rae, can you wiggle your toes please?'

Francis and Victoria stared at their daughter's feet as if nothing else existed on the planet, Rae wiggled her toes. Dr Vernon went to the monitor, made some adjustments, and came back round the bed to sit beside Rae again, nodding slightly at Francis and Victoria as she did so. She took Rae's right hand in hers and said clearly, 'Rae can you squeeze my hand please? Good.' She walked round the bed and took her left hand, 'And this hand? Good, very good.' She turned to Francis and Victoria and said, 'I know Mr Cameron was worried about a lesion affecting her left side, but she is responsive on both sides. We need to remove the ventilator now; it would be helpful if you left us with her for a little while please. Go and get a coffee.' It was more of an instruction than a request.

In the café Victoria sipped green tea and Francis drank black coffee. They were silent until Victoria said, 'What is it you think we are allowed to hope for now?'

'Everything,' Francis said 'That she can walk and talk, remember, think. Play guitar…'

'Laugh, run, swim…'

'Yes.'

'It might take time, but we have time.' Victoria said.

Francis felt a swell of something arrive in his chest. Where there had only been relief now there was something else, something filling him with a different kind of terror; the realisation that he did not have time, he had six months, and he could not tell a soul.

'Whatever it takes Vic, we have our girl back.'

'What did you do Francis? When you went away, you said she would be ok, and now…what.' She was staring at him through exhausted eyes, 'I don't understand,'

'You know what I love about you Vic? I mean there are loads of things but the one that stands out above everything?'

'Yes, I think I do, I love her as much as you do.'

'There isn't anything you would not do for her is there?'

Victoria was crying now, shaking her head.

'Me neither, whatever it takes Vic, we look after her, right?'

'No matter how long it takes.'

'No matter how long it takes,' Francis said, staring into his coffee.

*　　　　*　　　　*

In fact, it didn't take very long at all. Rae was allowed home after four weeks. Her pelvis had healed well and she had recovered to the point of becoming restless in hospital.

'There is no rush,' Mr Cameron told her, 'you are very good at healing, do not try to take advantage of that young lady.'

Rae smiled at him, 'thank you,' she said.

'You are welcome, sometimes we are lucky I think?'

On her second day home Joy came down to see her, when Francis opened the door Joy was holding a large box in one hand and had another at her feet. 'Give me a hand,' she said with a wink.

'I am so sorry, so sorry about the guitar Joy…I know…'

said Rae when Joy leant in to give her a hug.

'Shh you,' said Joy, 'I have bought you a new one, and your parents will be thrilled to know it comes with an amplifier.'

'But Uncle Ben made it and…'

'And it will always be the guitar you learnt on, so it did its job, and who knows, maybe it absorbed some of the impact, so it sacrificed itself for you, it was just a thing, a beautiful thing, but a thing. Now, let's plug this new thing in.'

Rae went tentatively back to school a month later. Her eye had healed, the lesion that Mr. Cameron worried about did not affect her, but the scar on her head was still visible, a reminder that there was still some healing to be done. When she came home from school on that first day she was smiling. The other students had made a banner welcoming her back, and in the morning assembly, when the head teacher said her name, everyone clapped.

In the evenings, after school, Rae would sit in her room playing the new guitar Joy had bought her, refamiliarizing herself with all the melodies and notes she had been separated from. Sometimes she plugged it in and when that noise came down the stairs Francis felt like the luckiest man who had ever lived. One evening, when he was upstairs, he heard her singing. Her voice was soft and she sang as though she were looking for something, perhaps the way all fifteen-year-olds are. *I wish I could hold on to this sound forever,* he thought, and he concentrated on remembering every note. *Where will this go, these feelings, this memory, this love, what will happen to it all when there is no me to hold it?'*

Victoria had come upstairs and she saw Francis leaning against the wall with a pillowcase in his hand, eyes closed, crying quietly. She turned around and went back downstairs.

It seemed to take Victoria longer to recover than Rae. She went back to work, but if she had been made thinner by the crash diet that was waiting for her daughter to open her eyes, and not eating anything more than an occasional fruit bar for two weeks, she had not even begun to put the weight back on. When they had dinner in the evenings she would pick at it, as if she had forgotten how to chew.

'You aren't eating,' Francis would say.

'I am,' she would say dreamily, and push a piece of pasta around a bowl.

Francis felt she had been drained of something. Victoria had always believed that most people are good, that you have a responsibility to work hard, help people if you can; that if you do no harm to others, no harm will be done to you. Rae being harmed had ripped that sense of order from her; she had become grey, less present, and she seemed to Francis wholly untouchable.

'The accident has changed you more than it has changed Rae, I think,' Francis said to her one night as they lay in bed listening to the rain and making sure there was space between them.

'Maybe,' she said dreamily. 'But I don't mind.' Victoria reached across the divide and stroked his arm. It felt as though she were absent-mindedly petting a cat. 'I'm sorry,' she said.

'What for?'

'For this.'

He knew exactly what she meant.

'And I am sorry you feel I left you at her bedside.'

'It doesn't matter.' She said and he didn't believe her.

'We are bound, the three of us,' he said. 'I wouldn't want anything else.'

'Wouldn't you?'

'No, would you?'

'No, but…we're different. Relationships…you know who I was. If I weren't with you, I wouldn't be with anyone, and sometimes that feels the most natural place.'

'Would you rather be alone?'

'No of course not, but if you met someone, wanted to meet someone, it's not like I wouldn't understand that.'

'I'm happy,' he said, wondering what he meant. 'Goodnight.'

Victoria always went to sleep quickly, and she was breathing heavily within five minutes, face buried deep, duvet pulled up tight for fear that the world might get in again and hurt her.

If I had more time, thought Francis as he lay there on his back, if I had twenty years, would I want anything different to this? But then all he could think about was Rae and the things that he would not see: her exam results, her first boyfriend or girlfriend, what she would be when she was seventeen, twenty or twenty-five. Would he choose to be anywhere other than near her if he had more days? Or as near as a dad can be to a daughter rapidly growing up? Watching, hoping, cheering her on, catching her if she fell? Was there a version of him that would rather be dating? Flirting? Getting to know someone new? If there was, he couldn't imagine liking that version of him. It wasn't an alternative future he wanted, it was just a longer one.

*　　　　*　　　　*

Three months after the accident they went on holiday to Crete.

'You used to talk about wanting to live on a Greek

Island, you said you would like to make a garden here. Do you remember?' Victoria said one evening in a Taverna overlooking a small, picturesque harbour.

'I remember,' Francis said quietly, 'the time has gone so quickly.'

'Most of it has,' Victoria said looking at Rae who was concentrating on her phone. 'Do you still imagine us doing that?'

'No,' he said abruptly. 'No, I don't.'

Later, back in the villa, after Rae had gone to her room, Victoria kissed Francis. It was tentative, nervous. He kissed her back with the same uncertainty and they began to slowly undress each other like teenagers who liked each other and feared what that might mean. They lay down like glass and made love like people who believed they might not make love again.

'Sometimes I pinch myself to remember I still have skin.' Victoria said afterwards.

'It's ok, Vic, it is ok now.' Francis said as he kissed her gently.

Victoria was crying, but when Francis tried to hold her, she instinctively pulled away before realising what she had done.

'I'm sorry,' she sighed, 'I just don't trust anything anymore.'

The next day they went to a small cove with a secluded beach that had a long shallow sandy slope into the sea. Francis sat on a beach towel and watched Victoria and Rae as they walked hand in hand down to the water. Victoria was sitting on the sand and letting the gentle clear waves wash over her legs while Rae swam and dived down for shells in front of her. Victoria could not take her eyes from her daughter and Francis could see the muscles in her back strain every time Rae disappeared under the surface, waiting anxiously for her daughter to bounce back up. He had less than three months left to live, then there would be just the two of them and when he looked at Victoria he knew that she would miss him, his presence, his companionship, his ability to do some of the jobs that needed to be done and his ability to make her laugh, but beyond that his absence would be another assault on her and her daughter. It would be the universe or the gods playing with them, hurting them, stealing from them. And he could do nothing to help her, to help them. He was spent now. He was useless.

'Fancy a swimming lesson?' He called instinctively. He stood up, walked toward them both, wanting to be close.

'Not remotely thank you, go and swim with your daughter, watch out for sharks and squids and stuff.'

Later that evening they were sitting in their favourite Taverna. Victoria and Francis were drinking wine and looking across the sea. Occasionally Rae would look up from her phone and say something random.

'Could you swim to that island Dad?' she said, nodding toward a large rock in the distance.

'Physically I could but the deep water would freak me out,' he said as he stared at the island wondering how far he would get before he panicked.

'You not going to ask me?' Victoria said.

Rae laughed and went back to her phone.

'You know,' Victoria said to Francis, 'I think I could live here, even if you couldn't.'

'Well, I would too then,' he lied.

She deserves to know everything, he thought, she doesn't deserve to spend the rest of her life wondering why I would leave that room. He decided then that he would write her a letter, to be read after he was gone, after his debt had been settled, after Rae's safety had been paid for.

'What if I didn't go to University?' Rae asked lifting her head from her phone again.

'What would you rather do?' Victoria said.

'Travel?'

'See how you feel,' Francis said, as neutrally as he could, but he squeezed Victoria's hand as he did so. Three months earlier their child had been in a coma; now she was talking about going backpacking or inter railing or simply wandering through other time zones without parental supervision. Victoria was not ready to imagine her child as an adult; she was still struggling to believe that she was repaired. Francis liked the idea: let her see things he had not seen, will never see; let her find her way, whatever that would be.

When it looked as though Rae had returned to her phone Victoria whispered, 'She isn't bloody going anywhere until she is thirty-five.'

Francis laughed. 'She is just trying things on, like she used to do with your shoes when she was four. It's nice.'

'What's nice about it? And don't pretend you'd be fine with her texting to say some cute boys have offered to give her a lift to Somalia on their boat.'

'I reckon she is just realising she is healthy Vic, just giving herself permission to wonder about life?'

'When did you get so relaxed?'

'Relieved, not relaxed. When I worry, I sort of remind myself that worrying about her future is a luxury we would both have given body parts for weeks ago.'

She patted his knee. 'Yeah well don't imagine for a moment I don't know that you would don a disguise and follow her if she went off travelling, and I would come with you.'

What a wonderful alternative to being dead that would be, thought Francis.

And Rae, with her eyes still fixed on her phone, said, 'And, when you've both finished, I want a tattoo like Joy's for my eighteenth birthday.'

20

Rae and Hannah were upstairs, playing guitar, chatting, laughing. Rae seemed to be thriving; it was as if the accident had jolted her gently toward people, rather than as Francis had feared, further from them. She was still not what anyone would call gregarious; rather she had a few friends and they were quiet together, but they seemed to laugh a lot and hug each other which Francis thought was sweet. She still played guitar most days, sometimes she left the door of her bedroom open, and they could hear singing. Rae was happy, Victoria remained grey, Francis had weeks left to live and had not told a soul.

'So,' Victoria said over dinner. 'It seems that people at work have noticed I am not quite myself and much to my surprise they want to do something about it. They have got together and bought me an early fiftieth birthday present, a weekend in a posh spa.'

'Just you? On your own?' Rae asked, 'because that suggests they just want to get rid of you.'

'No not just me on my own thank you, Jackie and Anne

from work are going too, it's not really my sort of thing…' she hesitated, not looking at either of them,

'When?'

'Half term, beginning of November.'

'Maybe it should be your sort of thing Vic?'

'It feels a bit funny being away from home?'

'We'll cope,' smiled Francis.

'I did think it might be nice,' she said, as if nice was a stranger that had wandered in and was hovering above her tapping her on the shoulder.

'They have pools, you know that right?' said Francis.

'It isn't compulsory to get into any body of water big enough for you to fit in?'

'Go mum, it would be good for you. You deserve something nice. I think the accident was harder for you two than it was for me.' Rae said decisively.

'I don't think that is true…'

'I do' said Rae seriously, 'you had to watch, I would hate to have to watch either of you be very sick. I was just asleep.'

Sometimes Francis could see the glimpses of the grown up she would become. Or at least he noticed them and called them signs; thoughtful, generous, perhaps insightful?

'I agree Vic, you deserve some pampering and the whole point of a spa is to soothe isn't it?

'What about you though?'

'What about me?'

'Well maybe you need something…I don't know, soothing too.'

'Swimming soothes me, going to work soothes me. Let's face it, I get a lot of soothing.'

'Can we stop saying soothing now?' Rae said.

Francis didn't want to be away from his family for one minute of the time he had left, but he also did not want to drop down dead in the kitchen. If Rae didn't want to see either of them sick then she certainly wouldn't want to be watching as one of them died. He wanted to be as far away from his family as possible come November 7th. He wanted them nowhere close when he died.

'Actually, there is something I would like to do, you know, if we are treating ourselves, something I have been thinking about since Ben died.'

'What?' asked Victoria.

'I would really to go to New York for the weekend, I'd like to see the garden that Ben read about, the one he based the trellis on, we talked about going together, they have all sorts of really interesting things going on there. They have artists exhibiting, installations, they have volunteers making up food boxes for local people, visitors are invited to work the garden with the people there.'

'You spend your life gardening and want to go and look at a garden,' laughed Rae.

'It's a bit different to anything I have seen or done, more developed, it is meant to be beautiful, I looked it up after Ben showed me the pictures. They grow lemons there and oranges, and…they really shouldn't be able to. I would like to see it before I…before it becomes…'

'Disneyfied?' said Rae.

'Yes, Disneyfied. Or taken over by Twitter or something.'

Victoria stared at him and he wondered if he had said something wrong.

'Am I being selfish? Is a weekend in New York more expensive than a Spa? Would you two like to come?' He felt sick when he asked the second question.

'Of course you aren't being selfish, but also, of course we don't want to come, do we Rae.'

'Can I make a suggestion then?' said Rae.

'As long as it is soothing.'

'Shut up Dad. How about you go to New York the same weekend as mum goes to her Spa and I go and stay at Hannah's?'

Victoria went pale.

'Hear me out mum, I am nearly sixteen, I am healthy and happy, I think you are traumatised, both of you, especially you mum, but you too dad, you walk around sometimes like there is a cloud following you, you think I don't notice but I do. And you mum, you look like you are, well…like you are scared all of the time. I would really like to do normal things. I also think normal things where we all do different stuff and get together afterwards and talk about it would be…I don't know…really healthy?'

They both stared at her.

'I don't know Rae,' Victoria said.

'I think she is right Vic,' said Francis, 'I think she gets that from me by the way.'

'What, saying things that make me anxious?'

'No, well yes, but also being right.'

Victoria looked at Francis, 'I like the idea of you going to see that garden. Particularly if that was what gave Ben the idea for that trellis thing you grow stuff on at your college.'

'It was one of the last things he made.'

She reached over and squeezed his hand. 'That would be a great thing to do, maybe you should ask Joy if she wants to come with you?'

'Maybe,' said Francis knowing he would not.

'It is the week before your birthday though…'

'Perfect, it is my fiftieth birthday present to myself.'

'This is exciting,' said Rae, 'and you both have to bring something back with you. Dad, not a snow globe. Mum, don't steal anything from the Spa, you wouldn't do well in prison.'

'You wouldn't Vic, you'd be someone's bitch,' smiled Francis.

'I'd be a kingpin, or whatever it is they call the prisoners who run things inside, not that I have signed up for this… what shall we call it…therapeutic project?'

'Please mum, it is a good idea you know it is a good idea.'

'It is,' said Francis who felt quietly proud of his thoughtful daughter and gut wrenchingly sad that he had to leave her.

*　　　　*　　　　*

Three days before he left, Rae came to the college garden with Francis and he was delighted to be able to show her around and that she was actually taking an interest.

'These are the trees we planted for Ben, that is the trellis he made,' he said.

'That is cool dad, are those plums?'

'Yes, and pears, the pears aren't ripe yet. When they are we take them to the food bank, so they get fresh local produce along with the other stuff.'

'Do you grow enough? I mean I'm not criticising but it's not exactly a farm, is it?'

'No, in the scheme of things it's a drop in the ocean but…'

'But it's something.'

'Yeah, it's something and…it makes me feel like I'm doing something to remember Nanny.'

'Because she liked fruit?'

Francis laughed, 'because we were one of the families who got given food and that made her feel bad, I think, this is a way of...you know...'

'Giving something back?'

'Maybe'

'That's nice dad, but knowing Nanny I think she would have preferred it if you had handed out cake. She did like cake.'

'That is true, she did like cake.' He smiled.

Afterwards he took Rae to the café on the seafront for hot chocolate and for no reason other than it was true he told her that he thought she was absolutely bloody brilliant.

'I am brilliant,' she said and then handed him a flash drive.

'What's this?'

'Before I tell you, you have to promise to follow the rules I am about to give you, or I will take it back and we will never speak of this again.' She sounded very serious but was half smiling.

'I promise. What is it?'

'It is a flash drive with three songs on it. I wrote them. I would like you to listen to them, but only when you are out of the country. You can listen when you are on the big plane if you like, but only when you are away from England. You have to promise.'

'Ok, I promise. Wow, you wrote some songs.'

'And recorded them. I got a bit of help on two of them. I want to know two things: what do you think and most importantly, how do they make you feel?'

'Alright then.'

'Look Dad, I haven't played them to anyone yet but I am interested in what they feel like, not whether I play well...that does matter a bit, I think it is a bit rude to ask people to listen to what you do and then do it badly, but mostly, how does it feel.'

'I promise I will do that. Thank you, thank you very much for sharing them with me. I am…I don't know what I am… thank you.'

            ＊   ＊   ＊

Two days before he was due to fly to New York, the three of them went out for an early dinner.

'What do you want for your birthday?' Victoria asked.

'Whatever you can find in the Spa giftshop?'

'Fluffy dressing gown?'

'Slippers,' said Rae.

'Or whatever is in the sale,' Victoria said.

'Keep the receipt,' Francis said, 'just in case it doesn't fit or something.'

They spent the evening laughing at each other, Rae and Victoria excited by the upcoming adventure, Francis desperately trying to soak up every drop of them both.

That night Francis didn't sleep. *This is nearly the last time I will lay here, how ridiculous is that?*, he thought, and he had to stop himself from waking Victoria to tell her that he wasn't coming back and that there were two letters on the computer desktop, a short one for her and a very long one for Rae marked, *In the event of me being seized by a triffid in New York.*

'Don't worry about getting up early or coming to the airport,' he'd said to them as they ate dinner the night before he left, 'it's an early flight and prolongs the goodbyes.' But when he got up at four in the morning to leave the house, Vic got up as well, to see him off. Rae slept on and he looked round her bedroom door before he left.

She looked younger when she slept, still a child. When she was little, very little, she would not go to sleep without one of them sitting with her making up a story or drawing pictures on her back with their fingers until she guessed what it was. He had seen her then, and almost every day since. He had not died when she was three or seven or twelve. He had seen her through the accident. She had felt loved.

He would not see who she would become, but she will become it nonetheless and he had her songs on a flash drive to listen to when he was over the sea. If it hadn't been for those, he might not have been able to close the door.

'Make sure you spoil yourself at the Spa, Vic' he whispered, 'and don't go in any pools without a big rubber ring and arm bands.'

'Wouldn't both be a tad excessive?'

'Not for you no. Kiss Rae for me.'

'Of course. Travel safe.'

If there was a part of him that wanted to tell her his secret, to let it all tumble out before he left, he held it in, not only because of the overwhelming superstitious fear that if he told anyone of his contract with the swimmer, at least until it was paid, it would be rendered void. But also because if he told Victoria what he had exchanged, and told her that he kept it from her in case that put Rae in danger, she would stare at him and say, 'So why the fuck are you telling me now? What if something happens to her now, you bloody idiot.'

21

He got an upgrade and extra legroom. *Look at me,* he thought, *flying to New York with my long legs, just sitting here in Premium Economy…waiting to die,* and he wondered if this was the universe giving him the equivalent of a last meal before execution. He took brief comfort in the passing idea that the universe was organising his death with some polite attention.

As soon as the seat belt signs were off, he got out his laptop, plugged in Rae's flash drive, and listened to her singing to him.

She had an interesting voice. It wasn't powerful: quite the opposite, it was close to fragile, it made him lean toward it. Her phrasing was nice, intimate, considered, and the music was layered if tentative; careful at first, almost coy. He was halfway through the first song when he realised she was singing about the man who drove his van into the café. The song was called *Meteorite.* 'You weren't even real,' she sang, 'a skin full of small disappointments.'

The second song was faster. She had overlaid guitars on it and sung some harmonies. It was quite poppy; it made him smile, he was tapping his foot. She sounded as though she was having fun

The last song was rock and roll: fast, tribal, somebody was beating the shit out of a drum kit, and someone was playing crude bass really loud. It was a *boys are stupid song.* It was funny, boisterous, young. He played them all again, noticing the occasional mistake, some youthful words and a different voice in the background, a harmony: two voices, one was a boy. He would text her when he landed, he would say, 'Listened, moved, may have danced to the third song which was embarrassing due to being on the big plane. Have you written more?' But he knew he would not hear anything else she did, and that thought kicked him in the middle of his chest and made it hard to breathe.

The time on the plane passed more quickly than usual, partly because all time did now and partly because he was in a comfortable seat, so he slept for a couple of hours. The queue through passport control was long and slow and the taxi to his hotel loud and disorientating. New York felt like a city swollen by life. It was a place where everyone seemed very serious about whatever it was they were doing, including his taxi driver and the man who checked him in at the Philadelphia Hotel opposite Madison Square Garden.

He did not want to stay in the small dark room and stare at the walls but before he went out he listened to Rae's songs again. He texted her his message and stared at the screen, waiting for a reply before remembering that she would be at school now.

He went out for a walk. The streets were wide and busy, everyone, it seemed walked fast in New York, everyone had somewhere to be and was racing against time to get there. He fell into step, trying not to get in the way of people, many of whom looked cross. *Of all these people, the hundreds of them, the thousands of them, would any one of them die before me?* He still clung to the strange comfort that was knowing that billions of people had lived and died before him. What was coming for him came to everyone, if he thought of himself as just another human, empty of the things he felt, loved, desired, if he thought about how tiny his existence was, that he was simply a passing soul, just a bubble in the universe, then it became bearable, for a short while at least.

He found himself in Central Park and it was pale and ordinary; it looked to be a large lawn where people came and ate sandwiches. He could appreciate how it had been planned, trees lining the undulating paths, flower beds punctuating the pale green of the grass. He had worked in places like this when he had started gardening, he had planted to the templates of large green spaces and someone had told him – it may have been William, the man who left to grow dahlias – that parks are designed as relief from the city, that they are like a trailer for nature, not nature itself. That was nearly thirty years ago, it was different now, parks were innovative, experimental, exciting. He knew that Central Park had corners and crevices that did bold and exciting things although he didn't know where they were and had no inclination to search them. He wondered briefly if William was still alive, *he'd be in his late seventies now,* he thought, and then quickly pushed it away, forty-nine is no age.

He kept walking, moving helped. He followed a path that led to the Metropolitan Museum of Art but didn't go in. Instead, he turned around and walked back the way he came.

He had been the link between Rose and Rae. Perhaps he had done nothing more than that and that was enough. His mother had lived like a shadow; always behind the light, afraid of everything until he had existed and for her that was all he needed to do. Who he became, how he lived; the things that she had told him mattered, that he imagined were important, they were just the incidentals of life. He existed and in so doing Rose had purpose and perhaps that purpose, his purpose, was to join everything that went before him to Rae.

Rae; vibrant, alive, so beautifully alive. He had simply been the link from woman to soon to be woman. That job was done. *If you want meaning, if you need your life to make sense; there it is, you were a bridge between good, good people, who knows what will come next,* he thought, and then, *but when she needs me I won't be there.* That thought crashed down on him like a freak wave.

His breathing became shallow and he was sweating. He wondered if he was about to have a heart attack, slip into a coma overnight, die in the morning. He felt afraid and lonely and sad. He sat on a bench, opposite a large ornate fountain. He closed his eyes and listened to the water, his breathing began to feel normal, calmer. He opened his eyes and when he saw that nobody was looking at him, he wondered if perhaps he was already dead. Maybe at the beginning you walk with the living, fade out of view slowly, see but not be seen.

That evening he walked down to Greenwich Village and bought pizza and cold beer from a shop next to a floodlit basketball court. On the way back to the hotel he bought himself a doughnut and coffee and went back to his hotel room. He planned his journey to the Honeycomb Garden and texted Victoria, 'Went to Central Park. It's a big lawn with monuments'

'I know how you love a nice lawn,' she replied sarcastically.

'They could grow all kinds of stuff in there,' he said, acting in their own private play, offering her a punchline that only they would laugh at.

'Then it would be a farm.'

He smiled. Even though he knew that that was exactly what she would write.

'How is the spa?'

'Soothing xx'

He texted Rae, 'How you doing?'

'Good, about to watch a film x'

There was no conversation to be had there. She was with her friend. He smiled to himself and laid down, pretending that sleep would come easily.

*   *   *

The next morning he caught the subway with the early commuters out to Brooklyn. The train was crowded but quiet, people read papers or stared at their phones, they drank coffee, they closed their eyes and listened to music or podcasts through earphones. Nobody seemed surprised to be here, they had done this journey many times before. There was a sense, he felt, that everybody knew where they were going and what was going to happen. That they would arrive at their places of work, sit at their desk or cash register or don whatever overall they had and set about the tasks ahead, like they had on the other days. But they probably also knew that something unexpected would happen. They may fall as they got off the train, they may make a mistake and get shouted at, they may fall in love. *I'll miss the small surprises,* he thought, before losing himself in the thought of nothingness; it was the incongruence of collecting memories, love and hope for his death that troubled him the most. *It is not as if I am going to lay on a cloud and be comforted by the things I saw or felt. There is nowhere to take my memories too. There is nothing.*

He remembered one of the last conversations he had had with Ben.

'Do you believe in an afterlife?' Ben had asked and it had felt like a trick question. An invitation to suggest that when the shaking stopped and he decided to die he might find himself in a better place. With tools and endless wood.

'Heaven?'

'Anything?'

Francis had shrugged and looked at his hands in his lap.

'Me neither. I don't think whatever it is we think we are, this collection of experiences and thoughts and perceptions and fears, can find itself in heaven.'

'Why?'

'Because there is a limit, I think, to how long any person could tolerate themselves before they went completely insane.'

'My mother would say that God would make it ok.'

'With all due respect to Rose,' Ben said, 'that would make God a sedative.'

He was glad when it was time to get off the train and he could move again. He left the station and turned right, not because there was a sign to follow but because most people were going that way. He walked for three or four minutes before realising that he had no idea where he was or if he was heading in the right direction. He looked around for someone to ask but whilst there were lots of people walking on the same sidewalk, they were all moving faster than him and none of them seemed approachable. To the right there was a smaller street, and he noticed a few people walking toward it from the station, they seemed to be moving more slowly and so he crossed the road and walked in that direction. There was a woman, coming from the station wearing baggy, blue dungarees and a head scarf that pulled back her black hair, the dungarees were rolled up to reveal a pair of dirty work boots. She, he decided, had the look of a gardener.

'Excuse me,' he said, feeling ridiculously English and perhaps blushing to prove it, 'I'm looking for a community garden, Honeycomb Gardens? Am I close?'

The woman looked at him evenly, she was probably in her forties, slim, serious looking. 'Sure,' she said, 'we're close, I'm heading there, what's your name?'

'Francis,' he said as he fell into step with her.

'Kathy,' she nodded. 'What are you coming to the gardens for? We aren't much of a tourist attraction.'

'I've read about them, I teach horticulture in a small college and a friend built us a trellis like yours. He saw it in a magazine, I wanted to see the original. I'm from England…'

'I'd guessed,' she smiled, 'A trellis like a honeycomb? Like ours?'

'Yes,' he said, 'smaller I suspect, we don't have much room. We grow vegetables and fruit and flowers. The students do most of the work.' He felt embarrassed.

'You have a trellis like ours?' she repeated. 'I hope it is more robust, ours is falling apart. Who made yours?'

'A friend of mine made it, he was…very good with wood,'

'We have extended ours recently, we had a problem with heavy snowfall last winter and the weight pulled the trellis apart. It was an opportunity to renew the whole thing and to make enough space to wrap some of the trees in fleece.'

Francis had only seen the two pictures of the gardens

that Ben had showed him. He had expected a football pitch of allotments, with the trellis serving as a boundary. He was wrong. The garden was on a long steep hill divided by a snaking path marked by gravel and bark with a low wall that began at the top and twisted its way down the slope. It was made of flint and large stones, there was no cement holding it in place, but it looked solid enough to withstand the snow Kathy had talked about.

'Have a look around' Kathy said, 'take your time.' She pointed to the bottom of the snaking hill, 'there are apple and pear trees down there on the left, I am going to be there, we are beginning to wrap them for winter, it's a little bit early but we had a problem last year with maggots.'

Francis nodded, 'grease bands,' he said without thinking, still staring at the garden. 'Where is your trellis?'

'Excuse me?' she said.

'Where is your trellis?'

'No, before that.'

'Oh sorry, grease bands, that is what I do. Put some sticky grease bands round the bottom of the trunk, stops the mothers crawling up and laying their eggs. Saves the fruit for next year. Sorry, it's probably different here, none of my business.'

The American woman nodded her head. 'It's a community garden Francis, it's everybody's business. Thanks for the tip. When you are done, maybe you can come and help? If you have time. The trellis starts over there,' she pointed to the bottom of the hill.

The honeycomb trellis was tied to the flint wall, but it had come away and was bending forward, rigid and reluctant, like a child getting ready to dive into water for the first time. The wood was rotten and the plum tree attached to it had come away at the top. *It doesn't look like it was good to begin with, nowhere near as good as Ben's.* Francis thought, *in fact it's rubbish compared to Ben's.*

It was a nice garden, but it didn't move Francis. The college garden was tiny in comparison, it produced less, it was not as good to look at, nobody would take photographs of it and put them in a magazine but he missed it and he missed his students. He even missed the tiny gardens of Hackney and Brighton that he had planned, dug and slipped baby fruit trees into. This was not the same, it was just a garden on the other side of the world that nice people grew things in.

He wandered over to a man who was standing beside a shed.

'I thought I would have a go at mending that trellis and sorting out those trees?' he said. The man looked at him evenly and nodded.

'Some tools in here,' he said as he stood aside so that Francis could take what he needed.

After Francis has finished with the trellis and the pear tree, he spent the rest of the morning helping with the apple trees because he wasn't sure what else to do with the last forty-eight hours of his life. At lunch time Kathy and some of the other gardeners said they were going to go and get some lunch and he walked with them, wandering through some side streets before emerging near the river. The water looked thick, deep and chunky and the river was wide. About a mile to his left was a bridge, beyond that, in the distance was another. *I could just get in and go. Go until I couldn't go any further.* He was too scared though and so he took a deep breath and turned back to his hosts.

'Do you sell small fruit trees?' he asked Kathy.

'Yes, but they won't let you take it through customs.'

'I know' Francis smiled 'but I would like to buy one anyway, something that can be planted in New York in November?'

'Sour cherry is your best bet,' she added with a smile, 'you need to borrow any tools?'

*   *   *

He waited until it was dark. He had a sense of how ridiculous he was. It was the day before he was due to die. Perhaps the gods might take him early, there would be nobody to complain if they did, nobody to ask for a rebate or compensation, and if they did, he was offering them the perfect opportunity. They used to say that Central Park was dangerous after dark, a place full of crime, but New York had changed, it was safer now.

There was a light drizzle when he left the hotel. He clutched a carrier bag with the baby cherry tree in it, small enough so that only a few tiny leaves poked out of the top and he had the trowel he had borrowed from the garden in his jacket pocket. He half expected to be stopped and asked where he was going with a tree in the middle of the night, in the middle of the city. But nobody spoke, nobody even looked at him.

When he reached Central Park he followed a path that ran eastward toward a wooded area, where the day before he had a group of bare cherry blossom trees. There was a dog walker coming toward him but otherwise the park was quiet. He put his head down and stepped off the path, reasoning that muggers rarely bring dogs out with them. He moved further into the wooded area until he was standing beside one of the cherry trees, he knelt down on the earth and began digging a small hole. He took the tree from the bag, dropped it in to the hole and gathered the soil around it. *Number forty-eight Rae*, he thought. He stood up, took out his phone and took a picture of it. Even with the flash it wasn't very good. *She would never find it*, he thought. *I should have brought something to bury beside it, to mark it*, but he had nothing. He would text her to tell her where it is when he gets back to the hotel and joke about his guerrilla planting. He would tell her to put it on the map he insisted on keeping. She would smile, shrug, consider it silly because it was silly but, as he stepped back from the tree he thought, *if there was only one thing left to do, I choose this.*

He walked slowly back to the hotel and when he got to the street it was on there was a man standing on the other side of the road singing, *God Bless The Child, badly.*

22

And now he was home. They had baked him a cake: a honey cake, his favourite. They ate it together when he arrived from Reykjavik the following day. He had slept badly in the airport hotel, confused by the incident on the plane, in some state of low-lying shock, worried that he was overdue on his payment and that he faced the threat of repossession, worried that Rae was not safe.

'I thought I was going to die,' he said to Vic that night.

She put her arms round him. When he put his hands on her skin, he felt more real again. When they kissed it was her smell that reminded him fully that he was still on the earth.

'It's ok, you are here now, it's all going to be all right,' she said.

But Francis didn't know that it was.

'I've always just wanted to look after my family, Vic,' he whispered.

'I know,' she said softly. 'We look after each other.'

'I always felt it was my job, with my mum, you know… and…when Rae was…'

'I know,' she said quietly. 'But she is good. We are good.'

We are, he thought, but he was alive and he was not meant to be. What sort of protector did that make him?

That night it took him a long time to fall asleep and when he did he dreamt he was in the sea again. It was rough and it was night but he could see lights on the shore, so he began to swim toward them. They were a mile or so away, he felt natural in the water, until it occurred to him that he might forget how to swim. As the thought tumbled through him, his stroke became worse, his body began to sink, he was forgetting how to be in the water and the terror that came with that thought was killing him. He woke up as the lights on the shore faded from view.

'Shh,' Victoria said. 'It's just a bad dream…you haven't had one of those for a while, it is ok, I'm here.'

She went back to sleep, but Francis lay awake. Fear is most intractable at night-time and he didn't fall back asleep until the sun had begun to come up. It was Saturday, Rae was still in bed and Victoria had gone out early to the shops. Francis ate toast, drank coffee, stared out of the window and finally he went to the beach. He thought a swim would help, but the water was grey and lumpy and the enforced break he had taken from the sea made him look at it differently. Every part of his body felt as though he were waiting for something bad to happen, half braced, half holding his breath, wholly on the lookout for traps. He thought about Victoria, how they had been slowly crawling back toward each other, healing and watchful. He thought about what he had said in the letter he had written to her and posted from New York, two very long days before. The one that told a truth he couldn't bring himself to say out loud now for fear it would crack his universe. Nothing makes you lonely like a secret. And he was lonely now, lonely and scared, and he realised he was angry too.

He phoned Victoria, 'I need to go to Birchington.'

'Why?' Her tone was soft, neutral.

'It is really hard to explain Vic, please bear with me?'

'Ok.' He could almost feel her shrug.

'There is something I need to do.'

'In Birchington?'

'Yes, in Birchington.'

'I don't understand the secrecy, Francis. It feels…it feels aggressive.'

'Aggressive?'

'Yes, like an assault, like you are filling the good space we have with something else.'

'Please just trust me. I will explain everything when I get back. I…' he ran out of words.

'I have to go,' she said, 'drive safe.'

He drove slowly, aware of the light-headedness that came with tiredness and a vague sense of wonder at the sun and the clouds. 'Unexpected days,' he said quietly to himself, and he found himself thinking of the tree he had planted in Central Park, wondering if he could go with Rae to find it in five, ten, maybe fifteen years' time. *Am I allowed to think things like that now?* He thought, thinking it nonetheless.

When he arrived at the beach at Birchington the sun was behind thick dark clouds but there was enough light to see the water stretching outwards. He parked his car as he always did, so it was directly facing the sea, and when he turned the engine off he could feel that it was cold outside. Close to the beach were just a few ripples of shallow water too tired to make a noise as they petered out on the sand and further out to sea there was a light chop, revealed by the shards of weak light that peeked through the grey sky. As he looked outward, the water got darker until it met the lighter sky to form a horizon. Conditions were quite good for a winter swim, he knew it would get a little rougher as the tide came in, but he sat in the car and stared at the horizon, ridiculously certain that he would be there, because whenever Francis had come, the swimmer had been there too.

He took his swim bag out of the boot and walked slowly to the slope on the east side of the beach, where he had exited with the swimmer the last time he had visited. He walked along the promenade and sat at the foot of the slope watching the tide slowly come in.

Francis had been watching the sea for nearly an hour when he saw the red cap and the distant splashing of a swim stroke emerge into sight. It took another twenty minutes for the swimmer to traverse the length of the bay and begin to wade in.

'Are you going in or have you already swum?' asked the swimmer as he sat down next to Francis.

'Neither, just watching. I came to see you.'

'That's unexpected.'

'Yes, I thought so too. Can we talk?'

'Of course. Talk to me. I can listen and dress at the same time. I'm smarter than I look.'

'It is November 9th, it is past my deadline.'

'Yes, you have a birthday coming up don't you?'

'Yes, will I see it?'

'I can't see why not.'

'I'm still alive.' Francis said starkly, staring at the old man.

'So I see…and now you are wondering what happened.'

'Yeah…and more importantly, what happens next?'

The swimmer was drying himself quite roughly, his head

down, staring at the ground. For a moment Francis wondered if he had forgotten he was there.

'I'm worried in case anyone thinks I did not fulfil my part of the contract in some way. Was I supposed to kill myself?'

'Don't be stupid. Nobody is ever supposed to kill themselves.'

'So what?'

The swimmer didn't speak. He put his towel round himself and started peeling off his wet trunks.

'Was it some sort of…trick?' Francis asked. 'Was it…just your way of trying to help?'

'Do you mean, did I make contracts with you that were just made-up nonsense? Ways of making you feel as though you were doing something to save the people you loved but were really just words between swimmers?'

'Yeah.'

'That would mean that Rose's recovery when you were little and Rae's recovery later would have happened anyway and had nothing to do with you.'

'I'm ok with that if it means my daughter is safe.' It wasn't until the words were spoken that Francis thought about what he was saying. *Am I?* he thought, *my whole life lived in the shadow of a lie, but I don't mind?* But it was true, just so long as Rae was going to be alright. He hesitated, realising that he was still bargaining now, still willing to offer whatever was required to keep Rae safe. A lifetime of delusion? Fine. Even if he was offering it to an old man on the beach who just made things up.

'That would be cruel, I think?' The swimmer said.

'Who are you?'

'I'm just an old man you met when you were a boy. I swim.

Always have. Always will.'

'I'm scared,' Francis said.

'You were always scared, son. You were when we first met, you were when your mum got ill, and I don't think you stopped being scared when she got better did you?'

'Not straight away.'

'Not ever. The universe is a chaotic place, bad things happen, quite randomly. They happened to you when your dad died and then your mum got ill and something even more random came along, me. And I like to think that was a good thing, but everything that comes after that is built on very shaky ground, isn't it? Leaves you waiting for the earth to open up and…and then it does and it launched an assault on your daughter…I think some people go through life never expecting anything to go wrong. You? I think you were waiting for the sky to fall in. I suspect that's why you didn't want to come down the stairs son.'

'How did you even know…?'

'I think you needed some type of control, Francis, when you were little. Maybe we all do. I think when it came, it calmed you, just a little?'

'Was it all pretend? Was it some kind of…intervention?'

'I didn't say it was pretend, I said that maybe the feeling of being able to do something helpful was useful to you.'

'Sounds like an intervention.'

The swimmer shrugged. 'I'm not sure I know what one of those is?'

'I hate interventions.' Francis mumbled

'Ok.' The swimmer turned to him slightly so that Francis could feel the old man's breath as he spoke. 'Well, there is another possibility…something that you might not have taken into account…'

'What other possibility?' Francis asked.

'Francis, you have done nothing wrong,' the old man said softly. 'You have tried to do the right thing, even when it must have seemed ludicrous.'

The sea was rolling in now, a swell was developing, and they could hear the waves breaking on the beach.

'Thank you, but doing the right thing doesn't make a blind bit of difference if it doesn't lead to the right outcome, I need to know that Rae will be…'

'Rae will be fine. The terms of your contract were met.'

'Why? How?'

'Does it matter?'

'Yes, it really, really does.'

The old man turned and faced him. 'Someone else made a deal, Francis. In the same way you gave up years to save Rose and Rae, someone gave up years for you. You are not the only person I have ever swum with. Nor the only person who gets to give something up for somebody they love. You have loved well; and you have been loved.'

Francis stared blankly at the swimmer. 'Who would do that? Who could do that?

The swimmer said nothing.

'That would mean they would have to know that I had… I had an arrangement.'

'Would it? Why?'

'How or why could they give something to save me if they didn't know I would need saving?' His voice was raised now.

'Everybody needs something.'

'What?' he shouted.

'Protect Francis when I can't. Protect him from himself or

worse. Please. That is all they would have needed to ask for. And then they would need to offer something in exchange.'

'Offer what?'

'Francis, really, that is none of your business.'

'I think it is…'

'How other people love? No. no it isn't.'

'Who?'

'Why don't you just go and live your life. Don't ask questions I can't answer.'

'How long do I have?' Francis was staring into the old man's damp grey eyes.

'People don't usually know how long they have, why don't you just try living with that, see what it's like?'

'Because that luxury was taken away from me when I was twelve and now I'm being given a future I'd not expected or planned for. This is one hell of a sarcastic universe. I don't even know you, I don't know your name…or anything. But you are there, at the middle of things. Even when you aren't… even when I don't see you. How am I meant to trust anything? I always imagined that it was important that I keep this all a secret. That there were rules somewhere even if I didn't see them or know them…'

The swimmer nodded his head once.

'I always believed that if I told anyone, it would render it all null and void, you know?'

'I never said that.'

'I know but…'

'I think you made your own rules, son. I think we all do. For what it's worth I think you made good rules.'

'I wanted to tell Victoria, you know…I wanted her to know that…that when I wasn't there it was for a good reason.'

'Haven't you already told her?'

'No, I haven't. But I told Ben, and soon after that he died, then Rose got ill again and I thought…'

'That you had somehow killed your mother.'

'No, of course I didn't think that' Francis said angrily. 'But I might have felt it.'

'I'm surprised you didn't tell Victoria. Love makes allowances.'

Francis listened and waited for relief to come but it didn't. The words just bounced off him like the waves bouncing back off the sea wall. Of course, it wasn't always about him, that would be stupid, his was an ordinary life. He was a gardener who loved his family, that was all. Yet somehow this man, this swimmer, these gifts had led part of him to believe he was more.

'The debt is paid then?'.

'Yes,' said the swimmer.

'But it doesn't feel paid.'

There was a break in the grey cloud that made the water glisten. I'll never come here again, he thought and then he said it out loud.

'I don't blame you son.'

Francis took off his jacket.

'You going in after all?'

'Yeah, I think so, before I head off, one last time'

'Fair enough,' said the swimmer. 'I might sit here and watch you for a while, see if you have learnt to swim properly yet.'

Francis fixed his eyes on the sea and put on his hat and goggles. He waded in up to his thighs and then turned round and got in backwards, all the while looking at the swimmer sitting on the promenade. He gave his breathing a moment to adjust to the cold water and then kicking his legs he propelled himself backwards over the incoming waves. When he turned to swim his stroke felt good, he was low in the water and the waves cut across him, but he kicked harder and stretched out and swam. He punched down into the water, let his leading arm glide and catch, every stroke felt strong, pulling him forward. He counted fifty, sixty, seventy strokes then he stopped counting and accelerated even more. He was swimming into the swell, strong, streamlined, fast, and then as he looked over his shoulder to see how far he had come something caught him in the chest.

He didn't know what came first, the feeling or the thought. He did know how to name them both though, just as they collided with each other. The feeling was terror: breathless, electric, lonely terror. Did he imagine that one swim to save his daughter had cured him of that? And the thought, riding on that uncontrollable fear was the letter. Vic would be getting his letter and it wasn't relief that accompanied that thought but panic. Now, in the bouncing, swell of the sea that danced around him, he was full of two things: terror and failure. The terror stripped him of volition, and the failure was as heavy as lead.

He stopped and looked toward the land, the sea was rising up in front of him, he turned away, back out to sea and as he did so a wave hit him hard in the face. He inhaled water and gasped, desperate for just a little bit of air in his lungs. He inhaled through his nose, feeling droplets of sea hitchhiking in on the air; and he gagged and retched and turned away from the waves, mouth open, desperate to be sick. His body shape was changing in the water, his legs sinking, he was becoming upright and he knew he needed to dip his head and adjust his weight so he was on top of the waves again, he knew what to do, he did this every day, and so he dipped forward and began to swim, the swell lifting him and dropping him down again. *Just get to fifty strokes, or seventy or a hundred and you will be close enough*, he told himself, but when he got to sixteen and he looked up he was even further away from the shore. He couldn't breathe through the fear, all reason had now been washed away, it was dark, his goggles were fogging up, and there was nothing but grey and the noise of an encroaching sea. He was crying and he couldn't breathe. 'Just swim,' the swimmer had said, 'the water will hold you.' When had he stopped believing that?

*   *   *

Francis felt a large hand on the top of his arm: gripping him tightly, it seemed to lift him unevenly. He was crying, he wanted to resist the hand that was holding him, but it was too strong, he was desperately looking for air but had nowhere to put it. He felt a slap on his back, a big hand, firm, very hard, like a punch, he coughed. He felt the arm pulling him, outward he thought, into deeper water, and he tried to resist again.

'Swim, just swim, on your back if you like, but swim, until you can breathe properly then just swim some more.'

He trusted the voice, this constant. He could breathe a little now and so he tapped the old man's hand and nodded, he turned on to his front and began to swim, breathing to one side, seeing the swimmer every time he turned his head to inhale, synchronising his stroke to the old man beside him. He swam until his hands touched the shingle beach, as they had when he was a child and his father had taken him there.

'What the bloody hell were you playing at?'

Francis couldn't answer, the seawater was still gurgling at the bottom of his lungs, and he was kneeling on all fours, retching into the shallows..

'Do you want to die? Is that it?'

Francis shook his head and pointed at his throat.

'Bloody stupid, you should know better. You were given a *gift*, a gift and you treat it like this?'

Francis had found himself where he had never dared to imagine, back in the middle of his wonderful, ordinary life. He had time in front of him, time with his family, with Rae, and yet he had got into an unfriendly sea and swum, until he couldn't. There was something left undone, he had no idea what that was but he needed to be sure. He had needed to surrender.

He stood up, head bowed, and waded out of the water and up the beach, the swimmer beside him, marching like an angry, disappointed parent.

'I'm sorry,' Francis said, too quiet to hear. The wind bit into him now, he was shivering and lightheaded. He picked up his towel, rubbed it half-heartedly across his face and shoulders and sat down on the wet concrete, staring at the howling sea. He felt dizzy, and the rain was stinging his eyes, so he lay down on his side and closed them.

'I'm sorry...' he muttered.

'You need to stop trying to give things away.' The swimmer's voice was clear. 'And you need to get up, get dry and get dressed.'

Francis lifted himself on to one elbow, put his hand to his face and removed his goggles before laying back down on the cold hard concrete again and curling into a shivering ball.

'I worry...' he said.

'Shh...'

'I worry…all the time…'

There was a hand on him now, soft, small, and his towel was moving, drying him.

'Shh, come on, sit up, let's get you dry, get dressed, come on, Francis I mean it, come on now, you are freezing, this is silly, please…'

It was Victoria's voice, Victoria's hands rubbing the towel up and down him roughly, Victoria pulling him up to a sitting position.

'Vic?'

'It is raining you know, and it's November, come on, let's get a shirt on, and get those trunks off: there is nobody to see you, nobody else is stupid enough to come to the beach in this. Rae is in the car, she is scared, very scared she wants her dad, so put some bloody trousers on. Come on Francis, I can't do this on my own, help me, put your arm in this, help me, now. Quickly, you don't want Rae to see you like this. Where is your woolly hat, you always have a woolly hat.'

'Ouch' he said as she moved the arm the swimmer had grabbed, he looked at it, there was already a series of fingerprint bruises forming around his bicep.'

'That's going to look impressive tomorrow,' she said. 'Where did you get that?'

'It was where he grabbed me, pulled me out.'

Victoria looked past him toward the car. 'Rae is coming, she is crying, you made her cry Francis. She doesn't understand what her father is doing.'

'I sent you a letter.'

'It came this morning. That's why we are here.'

'I didn't know, if I told you, I didn't know.'

'I know, shh.'

'Daddy, what are you doing,' Rae had appeared beside them, her face was wet. She looked twelve. She had not called him daddy since before her accident.

'I'm alright sweetie, I'm sorry, I came to see someone, I'm sorry.'

'I showed her the letter Francis,' Victoria whispered.

'Why did you do that?'

'Because. Secrets. Not helping.' She was rubbing his head with the towel, half kindness, half assault.

'Daddy you shouldn't swim in the sea when it is like this. It's dangerous.'

'I'm sorry sweetie, I made a mistake, I'm sorry and I promise I won't do it again.'

Now the relief began to come, pulsing slowly through him with the blood that was beginning to flow again.

'You need to stop trying to pay debts you don't owe,' Victoria said.

'That's what he said.'

'Who?'

'What do you mean who, the swimmer, I'll introduce you now.'

But there was nobody there, just Francis and Victoria sat cuddled together on the cold wet concrete, and Rae standing in the rain looking out toward the horizon.

'I think I can see your friend Dad,' Rae said too quietly for them to hear.

Acknowledgements

This book came quite quickly although it needed a lot of refinement. It emerged from conversations with my mate Jamie. He had cancer and knew he was dying. We talked about what constituted a good life, about the feelings and residue that clung to working class men of a certain age, about what love looked like, about gratitude and responsibility, and we talked about fear. I miss those conversations and my friend very much.

I had much help beyond that of course. Kate is the most patient and supportive wife and Maia the most thoughtful and enthusiastic of daughters. I have benefited from the reading and feedback of Bonnie A Powell, Augustas Jackevič, Tilly Bones and my agent Nicola Barr.

Away from the words I swim a lot. Have done for years. I'm not great at it but it makes me happy so I plod up and down the Brighton and Hove coast in all weathers and I do it with a pod of like-minded, big hearted and soulful swimmers.

Anyway, I suspect this book and its preoccupations emerges from the swimming, the security and the simple and recurrent decency of a group of people who are just kind to each other near water most days.

Finally, I want to thank Sean Campbell for his skill, vision and integrity. As well as the rest of the team at époque press. And I feel compelled to add that I have benefited from being an accompanist to my MA students at West Dean College of Art and Conservation. Under the guise of being their teacher I learn from them all, all of the time.